STEPS
UNDER
WATER

STEPS
UNDER
WATER

A Novel

ALICIA KOZAMEH

Translated from the Spanish by David E. Davis
Foreword by Saúl Sosnowski

UNIVERSITY OF CALIFORNIA PRESS

Berkeley   Los Angeles   London

Originally published as *Pasos bajo el agua*
© 1987 Editorial Contrapunto

University of California Press
Berkeley and Los Angeles, California

University of California Press, Ltd.
London, England

© 1996 by
The Regents of the University of California

Library of Congress Cataloging-in-
Publication Data

Kozameh, Alicia.
    [Pasos bajo el agua. English]
    Steps under water : a novel / Alicia
Kozameh ; translated from the
Spanish by David E. Davis.
        p.   cm.
    ISBN 0–520–20387–9 (alk. paper). —
    ISBN 0–520–20388–7 (pbk. alk. paper).
        I. Davis, David E.   II. Title.
PQ7798.21.O9P3713   1996
863—dc20   96–13721
                                        cip

Printed in the United States of America
9   8   7   6   5   4   3   2   1

⊚ The paper used in this publication meets
the minimum requirements of American
National Standards for Information
Sciences—Permanence of Paper for Printed
Library Materials, ANSI Z39.48–1984.

This version in English,
for Jamee

Foreword

Of Memory's Literary Sites

Saúl Sosnowski

It could have taken place almost anywhere. But for a few
names and allusions, *Steps Under Water* could refer to experiences under any one of the dictatorial regimes that uniformed
the Southern Cone. Beyond Latin America, readers who have
experienced oppressive regimes will nod in sad recognition of
this tale of resistance and survival. Yet Alicia Kozameh chose to
disregard the openness of her novel with an epigraph that, as
she acknowledges, "seems redundant." In saying so, she clearly
admonishes us to tread cautiously on a context that traverses her
own life. Based on biographical material and a composite of
the author's *compañeras* in prison, this novel retrieves a cross
section of Argentina from the mid 1970s to the early 1980s. Set
in days and nights of lead and sorrow, of violence and institutional bankruptcy, Alicia Kozameh's fractured texts come together in a voice that evokes and, at once softly and stridently,
attests to violations of human and legal rights. Written with a

clear sense of purpose, the novel renders an eloquent homage to survival and to the memory of the victims.

By the time Isabel Martínez de Perón (Isabelita) was flown out by helicopter from the Pink House to a southern destination, Alicia Kozameh had already been imprisoned for six months. She would remain a political prisoner, first in her hometown of Rosario and then in Buenos Aires, until late December 1978. A militant in one of the organizations that sought to change the nation's social order, Kozameh was among the "lucky," among the "legal" prisoners who did not join the ranks of the thousands of disappeared. For prisoners, political consciousness and organizational discipline were a source of solidarity and pride, of resilience during beatings, of resourceful skills to endure their daily fare behind limitless bars. For the political prisoners, even in the jails that held common criminals, the 1976 coup would have a different meaning.

The event of 24 March 1976 relieved—or so many of its supporters initially thought—a vast segment of Argentine society from the nightmarish chaos that characterized the disheveled reign of Isabel Perón, of José López Rega, and of the terror squads of the Argentine Anticommunist Alliance. Right-wing terror, officially sanctioned terror—it was claimed—surged to forestall the so-called terror from the left, from organizations such as the leftist Peronist Montoneros (formed in 1968), the Ejército Revolucionario del Pueblo (ERP, active since 1971), and other, smaller, liberation forces. Dramatic social polarization, indigence, and injustice as root causes for violence did not seem to enter the equation in launching an all-out war against those who attacked or were perceived to attack the established order. "Subversives" was the generic term applied to the guerrilla forces by the very same accusers who subverted institutions, that is, the legal and ethical foundations designed at the inception of the republic and sanctioned by the 1853 constitution to sustain the nation.

By the time the coup took place, most of the guerrilla forces had been defeated. The authoritarian regime that ruled until 1983 sought to assure the establishment of a new economic order on the death and torture of thousands of dissidents, innocent bystanders, the changed identities of children born to the disappeared, the silence and acquiescence of a population that reaped financial benefits and said in unison of the taken, *Por algo será* (there must be a reason).

In order to understand the magnitude of these events, a brief recollection of a few names and events is necessary. The first name is that of Juan Domingo Perón, the elected populist general who ruled from 1946 until his overthrow in 1955, and who continued to influence Argentina's political life from exile and, once back in Argentina, even beyond his death. Perón's overthrow was not the first military action against a civilian government nor, as Argentines learned to expect, the last. Juntas traditionally claimed that their actions were forced upon them to defend their country's "national, Western, and Christian values" and, given their own transitional character, to guarantee the eventual restoration of a true democracy. Since 1955, and for a number of years, the military also aimed to prevent the return of Perón and his Justicialista party to power.

A retrospective look at the last thirty years clearly suggests that the 1966 coup that overthrew President Arturo Illia and brought General Juan Carlos Onganía to power was a major step in the socioeconomic as well as the political transformation of the country. It was during Onganía's regime, and particularly as a result of the 1969 popular uprising in Córdoba (the Cordobazo), that the country became even more cognizant of increasing and all-pervasive levels of violence that would climb to dramatic new peaks in the following years.

Negotiated political alliances and a certain commonality of purpose in the restoration of civilian rule between the military and the political parties, including Perón's representatives, led to a "Gran acuerdo nacional" (Great national accord) and eventually to the election of Héctor J. Cámpora. Throughout this period, and for years to come, the internal debates within Perón's following did not spare bloodshed. Perhaps the most eloquent evidence of the polarization among those who invoked Perón and Evita, and who ranged from the extreme left to the extreme right, was manifested in the violent eruption that greeted Perón's final return to Argentina on 20 June 1973. On 12 October Perón and Isabelita assumed power as president and vice president of the republic. In the midst of growing violence and internal conflict among Peronista followers, Perón was publicly rebuffed by Montoneros and the militant Peronist youth (*Juventud peronista*).

When Perón died on 1 July 1974, the reins of power reverted to his widow and to her close confidant, the president's private secretary José López Rega, commonly known as "el Brujo" (the sorcerer). The Senate acted to forestall the institutional collapse of the nation by imposing Italo Luder as provisional president. During his brief presidency, and while attempting to restore some semblance of constitutionality, he formalized the armed forces' actions against the guerrilla movements. Politics and military action became increasingly intertwined and public opinion was once again being readied for a coup to reestablish order.

The 1976 coup was promptly named by its perpetrators "Proceso de reorganización nacional" (Process of national reorganization). The junta's bulletins and edicts clearly indicated that this time the armed forces would go beyond the physical elimination of the opposition. The body of the nation had to be preserved by extirpating the cancerous cells that invaded its core. Once opponents are removed from the category of human and denigrated to a diseased object, their elimination is not only possible; it becomes mandatory. The rationale that designed the "Doctrine of National Security" was all-pervasive. As outlined by the juntas, the goal was to forestall leftist inroads that threatened the national character, to shape the country according to the values espoused by their own conservative principles, to establish a new economic order, and, at the same time, align the country with the leading combatants against international communism. While the junta headed by General Jorge Rafael Videla confronted the leftist guerrilla movements—and while violence from other sectors continued to rip through the streets—the Minister of Economics José Alfredo Martínez de Hoz informed the nation of Argentina's new order.

The two most visible legacies of the dictatorship are its gross violation of human rights and, in another realm, one of the world's most calamitous foreign debts. Fractures within the armed forces, the border conflicts with Chile, and the Malvinas/Falkland war with Great Britain—these failed results of many of the objectives that the junta outlined upon assuming power would finally put an end to the grimmest period of Argentine history. The formal transition to democracy began with a call to elections although throughout the period varying acts of resistance pushed back restrictions on civil liberties and censorship. Elections were held on 30 October 1983 and resulted in the unexpected victory of the Unión Cívica Radical's leader, Raúl Alfonsín and, consequently, for a brief time, in the resounding rejection of another Peronist government.

Among Alfonsín's most laudable accomplishments were the appointment of a National Commission of the Disappearance of Persons (CONADEP), which issued its report under the title *Nunca más* (Never again), and the subsequent trial of the junta's members. These momentous events signaled, albeit all too briefly, the return of an ethical imprint on the governance of the state. Subsequent laws to curb the number of the legally accountable for violating human rights and other crimes, and a presidential pardon—issued, respectively, by Presidents Alfonsín and Menem—marred those accomplishments. Political closure was in order to appease the restless among the armed forces, to forge ahead toward the first world, and to be firmly aligned with the forces of progress under the banner of a triumphant neoliberalism.

No such closure, however, could be accomplished with the victims' families without a full accounting of the disappeared and the trial of those responsible for the criminal actions outlined in *Nunca más* and in the trial of the members of the juntas. No further attempts were made to heal the nation. Those who suffered directly, witnessed by organizations such as the Mothers of the Plaza de Mayo, could not be appeased; political prisoners were offered monetary compensation; the rest of the population—as the leadership astutely and accurately calculated—would soon move on toward the more alluring specter of financial success or become more preoccupied with its own survival.

In spite of a recent reissuing of the *Diario del juicio* (Diary of the trial) accompanied by documentary videos, most Argentines are distant from stories that throw them back to the times of "victorious horror." Daily life, a political rhetoric that fills the present, and the fact that words uttered on those days carry a tacit accusation about a complicitous silence, suffice to explain such disregard for the country's recent history. Both temporal distance and the rationalization that violence had similar signs when it emanated from right-wing squads and state-sponsored terrorism as when it stemmed from guerrilla organizations (the misleadingly comfortable "theory of the two demons") also made it increasingly viable for the majority of the population to accept measures designed to leave atrocities and accountability as part of a past that (as many allege) has been overcome. Outbursts of indignation and ethical islands remain and will continue to exist, but these have been surrounded by the waters of expediency and cynicism.

Therein lies the significance of Alicia Kozameh's epigraph and of the novel's literary and historical importance. There can be no shortage of drama in a survivor's account but Kozameh's language renders excruciating pain in muted tones. It shifts from the deafening clang of tin cups against the prison bars to demand aid for an ill *compañera* to the soft tenderness of human warmth and a quiet slipping away into death. A discourse on ethics, on rights, is substituted by the begging defiance that makes life itself a challenge to arbitrariness.

Neither the core of authoritarianism nor the ideological tenets that led to the left's call to arms are evident in the novel. It engages the aftermath, daily survival after defeat as victory is sought in the very act of staying alive, of not surrendering to the jailer's imposed order. Epic actions are absent; they are part of an unmentioned legacy. The greatest possible epic within the cell is to survive. To guard the words that express resistance becomes the sole guarantee for a day after.

The preservation of language, notably under these circumstances, attests to the defeat of the authoritarian mind-set that imposed categories of exclusion and acted against citizens tagged as disposable. Literature should not be charged with the awesome burden of chastising readers into guilt and burdensome recollections. Neither should literature completely neglect the testimonial voice of the times. Bridging these daunting tasks, *Steps Under Water* succeeds in leading us into a world that too many have unjustly known and that many more pretend to ignore. We are witnesses to the rejection of oppression, violence, and life, as well as to the perverse joy of inflicting pain, of plundering, of sacking lives, property, and the future.

Perhaps a literary text should not be burdened with contributing to the preservation of memory, but a nation must hold its past, and particularly its most traumatic history, as a trust for future generations. The women who survived the penal colonies, the reasons for the struggle that led to bodies censored through torture and death and to repressive silence, as well as their triumphant resistance, are part of a legacy that *Steps Under Water* engraves in our letters and in our minds.

The first edition of *Pasos bajo el agua* (1987) reproduced the notebook cover that Alicia Kozameh was duly authorized to keep in her cell. Guarded words, however, could never account for a world that was to be kept from a knowing or suspicious public. Words that partake of the innermost intimacy of truth had to be hidden in the sole place that wasn't searched by prison wardens. In death and in life, the *compañeras'* bodies became safekeepers for memory and, for Alicia Kozameh, the renewed birthplace of writing.

January 1996
College Park, Maryland

A preface for this novel seems redundant. So I am going to force myself to locate that elusive capacity of mine for synthesis and say the following:

I was imprisoned on 24 September 1975, a few hours after my companion at that time. I was released to "freedom under surveillance" (another form of arrest) on 24 December 1978.

In April 1980, after the predictable intimidation and runarounds, I was finally able to obtain a passport that had been processed eight months earlier. During the first days of June I went into exile. California and Mexico.

I returned to Argentina in June 1984.

This was written so that these events would be known.

The substance of the story, of every episode, is real; it happened. Either I myself or other *compañeras* lived it. I have, however, replaced names or possibly details that in no way affect the essence of what occurred.

I don't think there is really anything else to add.

This story is dedicated, of course and as always, to all the *compañeras* who passed through the women's ward of the Rosario Police Station: the "basement." To the ones who went through Devoto. To all the *compañeros.* To the dead, the disappeared, and to the ones who were able to preserve themselves through years of hiding, of waiting. And to those who still remain in prison.

A.K., Buenos Aires, 1985

This book was originally published in Buenos Aires
in June 1987.

After 1984 there were, for the most part, no disappearances
or indiscriminate deaths in Argentina. A democratic
government was in place.

But the power still remained in the hands of the military,
with everything this implies.

My daughter and my writing were a source of great
satisfaction for me during those years in Argentina,
though I did experience pain, impotence, anxiety.

Following the publication of this book, I was threatened by
members of the Buenos Aires police.

In July 1988 I left Buenos Aires to reside once again
in Los Angeles.

A.K., Los Angeles, 1996

A Way Back

Sara climbs: she climbs the stairs running and once at the very top she looks out, over the patio of her parents' house. And in front of her, the terrace. Everything is at once firm and slippery, it's there and then it vanishes. Easier to turn it into one big lie: like a circus, for example. She settles on this new space with elephants and equestriennes. She imagines them and wonders if they would eat geraniums or sunbathe as she did, years ago, in that very spot.

Maybe this time her escape hasn't worked out. Escaping is an involved process. The more expert you are in the field, the easier it is to fail. To escape upstairs is to run smack into the question of how to get back down. Anyway, already busy with the task of physical recognition, she escapes, but throwing caution to the wind. Except now her circus vanishes as well and she can do nothing more than stop and hold onto the floor tiles, onto the faucet that pokes out of the wall like a snake's head. Onto the hose.

How many footsteps, she asks herself? By how many milli-meters had her mother's feet worn down the thickness of the floor tiles during those three and a half years? How many in-sects had been worked into the porosity of the floor by footsteps that ground them into that same spot, day after day? To know this would be enlightening. To ask, but to ask what. Why bother computing stupidities? I get so sick of thinking about everything in terms of numbers. Besides, nothing can ever be answered unless you've been there. You have to see, and then you get the answer.

What am I doing here, my body seemingly stuck to this ter-race, to this faucet, to this geranium, to this blue sky that's only meant to go with a river—all doing their best to convince me they're real when I know it's possible to block them out for years. To keep them suppressed.

And now what? Try to flex my imagination that's been nar-rowed by absence. Take another look at the way to appear in the world. In the car, on the way to this terrace, nobody asked me what I thought about the sun and the streets. The light or the rhythm of people's feet as they walk. The sounds of motor-cycles, the name brands that were so ingrained in the minds of certain persons—what did this stir up deep down? And I ask myself what my father and mother might think about what was beginning to circulate through my brain and my blood. I won-der what they imagine it's like to regain something all of a sud-den, to fill the emptiness with sounds that have never been for-gotten? They probably think there's nothing new about that. Or even better: maybe they feel like you can't recuperate what you never really lost. They just don't believe there was ever any dan-ger in being left with nothing. Nor would they believe I'm so resistant: resistant because everything that's surrounded me in the past few minutes chokes me with happiness and numbs me with anguish.

And that guy. The same one. But they wouldn't understand that either. It was the same one, only with different hair. It was no accident that he came through that door. In the summer, with Hugo's jacket. Wearing it. They all know who's being released. And they don't forget anyone, even though each one of them has a thousand to his name. The guy didn't even bother looking over at me, but he left wearing that jacket, just so I'd see him. And my parents don't believe that, they don't understand what that means. They don't want to recognize that vulnerability is a daily fact. And that it's not easy to neutralize it. Defend against it. But there's nothing to explain. What I have inside of me is all mine. And it takes me away to a solitude that I neither pursue nor resist.

Sara walks to the ledge and peers over and sees the street. Buses, people inside. Wonder where they're going. How many times they must have taken that same bus while I was away. Once again the numbers. And what good are they anyway.

She turns around. She wants to take in the full extension of the terrace. Why does it seem so small, she still insists with the questions. My sight got used to other spaces. And what does this matter.

Just then she hears a mewing and her nerves crackle. She doesn't scream out: she can't.

A cat. I wonder where it is. What do I do now, where do I hide? In which corner? She looks around, squinting her eyes. Why bother finding out.

There is a corner of the terrace where the sun doesn't reach;

the two yellowing walls and, at a right angle, you can see the tawny flagstones and the tubs holding the geraniums. She sits along the edge of the tub. My pants'll get dirty. So what? Now I'll try to think about cats. More and more I'm having fewer doubts about their existence.

They used to be soft. I'm sure they still are. Warm, strange. Their tails would swish back and forth. You could stick a cat in a box and observe it. Watch all its reactions. I'm sure my pants are covered with dirt. Now I'm just beginning to settle down. A flagpole. A cat is like a flagpole. Always stretching toward the sky, its eyes like a flag floating in its head. Cats live, die, then come back to life. Or they don't die and instead are spared from every kind of possible danger. Well, almost. Because I *have* seen dead cats. What a horror.

That first time, when Papa was carrying me around on his bike, on that little seat he'd fastened to the handlebars. I couldn't have been more than three. We were going to Alberdi, over to the house of my uncle, who back then was very much alive and who couldn't possibly imagine he'd get cut down in the street, just like so many cats, though from paramilitary bullets instead. We were passing by the power plant and I saw a dark shape moving around in the middle of the street. I asked my father what it could be and he told me, two newborn kittens, probably sick or dying. Right then I wanted that bicycle to go at death's speed. For the first time in my life I felt that horror invade me. Or maybe the first time was that baby sparrow down the block, around the same time. I don't know.

And that other white cat, at the door of the butcher shop, which was on the way to the piano conservatory in Laboulaye. Snow white. I must have been seven or eight. It was winter. Its mouth open. I ran like crazy. Every so often I turned around just to tell myself that I was far enough away not to see it anymore.

During that lesson I played the piano with abandon and got into a fight with the teacher because she made me follow along shamefully with the music in the books, and I told her, I want to improvise. I want to play what comes out of me. Last night I made up a song and now I want to play it. And the old shrew hollered at me. I got up from the bench and she sat me back down with a shove.

It's hot here. This terrace is burning up. But it will be night-time soon. These geraniums are streaked with different colors. I didn't know they were out here. I knew the red ones were. I remember those and the white ones.

And that one by the post office. Its eyes bugging out. Big and yellow. I saw it and couldn't bear it. I got sick to my stomach and collapsed. The old women who helped me up must have thought that only an idiot would faint at the sight of a dead animal. What could two old women know about the kind of things that go on inside a cat's body. I got home and my throat was all swollen, like its corpse had lodged itself there, fat and yellow. Between the tongue and the esophagus. I went straight to the bathroom and threw up.

So many years change dimensions, plant lies in the imagination, collude with forgetting. Well, with certain kinds of forgetting. I'd like to remember where cats go, besides the terraces.

What difference can there be between what a *milico** feels

---

*A pejorative applied to a member of the police, to a soldier, or to anybody in the armed forces.

when he sees a dead cat and what I feel now when I hear their mewing. Maybe an encyclopedia would help. I need to look something up about cats; find out once again, learn.

And the other one with the hole in its belly, crawling with ants. I felt a million needles jabbing into my head. OK, that's enough, enough.

A cat is like an orchestra: it shows up, rewards us with its music, and disappears. Have to survive those shocks. Get used to them. I have to assimilate each intensity little by little. Carefully. Whoever doesn't understand what I'm doing here among cats and geraniums has a right to be surprised, to gesticulate, to open his mouth, eyes, arms and to stand there like an idiot trying to ravel out the meaning of it all.

The doorbell has rung a number of times. It must be my friends.

It's too much to discover all at once that terraces and everything else actually do exist. The moon. You can see it. You have to dare to look at it. Which is hard when there's no possible way to share it with those who still don't have it within their reach. The moon and the cats.

Sara has the moon in her head. Her eyes glued to the floor. And then a cat strolls across the terrace, she loses her breath and then cries out, and the screams can be heard downstairs.

A cat, Papa. A cat. It wants to pounce on me. Claw me apart.

A cat strolls across the terrace.

Sara runs for the stairs. Her father is already at the top, trying to explain to her that yes, going years without seeing animals is not something to take lightly. But she should try to remember how much she liked cats, how as a kid her hands would break out in rashes from playing and rolling around with them.

He must be worried. He must think I'm completely mad. To him, a cat is an animal. It scares you, but what does he know about that. I have to take charge. Figure it out. I have to get them back. All that time I never had them around me, either dead or alive. I began today by seeing them alive.

"What were you doing up here all this time? It's getting dark."

"I was trying to make peace with the cats."

Her father stares at her, frowning.

"Let's go, honey. Come on down and see your friends. Cristina, Elsa, and Marco are here. They're waiting for you."

Sara follows her father down with the slowness you have to use on a stairway covered with sick cats, hanging, clinging from the banisters, soft or hard like dried rubber, if you don't want to step on them or touch them with your feet.

Prison doesn't give you time to think about cats; nor is there room to rehearse circuses or any other kind of escape.

For my father a cat is a cat. To me it is a gesture of mock reverence that freedom makes at me today. Take charge.

I stop. I walk, I stop.

The Facts: The Ditches

Last night she dreamed that they took him away and she warned him in the morning between matés*: Hugo, don't go to work. You won't come back. Of course he, very much a materialist and rightly so in this instance, gave her a hug, told her to stop her crazy nonsense, and handed her one last maté with coffee and sugar to see if she too could muster the necessary energy to pull herself out of bed. Sara kissed him, again insisted, and still he skipped out the door at five o'clock in the morning, as he did every day.

Sara observed how on his way out, before opening the door, he glanced at the mirror, looked into his eyes as if talking to himself, bit his mustache, studied a scar on the side of his fore-

---

*Yerba maté, an herbal tea cultivated in Argentina, Paraguay, and Brazil and traditionally served among friends. The herbal leaves (the "yerba") are put in a gourd, which is filled with hot water, and the maté is then sipped through a metallic straw.

head, flashed a half-hearted smile that was split in two by a crack in the mirror, and then abandoned the game.

It was now two-thirty in the afternoon and he should have been home by two. She returned from the street and began making vanilla custard, asking herself: for whom? I can't stomach the milk. Hugo isn't going to show. That lassitude began to overtake her; she didn't fight it. She went to bed and fell asleep on the covers, fully clothed.

She heard a pounding that seemed to come out of a pit of shadows. It's not Hugo: he has a key. Who then? And she knew. She sat up.

The door caved in.

They forced their way in and asked for Hugo. They laughed. She didn't answer. We know. We had to kill him. He tried to get tough and punched the skinny one over there with the gash on his forehead. And now he's lying in a ditch on Rondeau Boulevard. Show me where the guns are.

She imagined him dead. She was seeing a scene of rabid clowns unfold around her: the fat one was trying on one of Hugo's coats and ripped its sleeves—so it'll fit me—when the skinny little one landed the first punch in her stomach and the rest of them pounded on the floor and the walls, searching.

She saw what nobody else could see: suns that crashed through the ceiling and entered the room, cracking open and releasing red spheres, exploding and sending colored letters flying, letters that were no doubt uttering interminable phrases she couldn't quite read because they vanished, and the suns would return again, with each successive blow. She hardened her stomach but it wasn't enough—so much pride about her thin figure only now to have them bury their fists clear through to her back.

They asked her questions, they interrogated her for an eternity. An eternity of red-hot stones.

They broke the legs off the bed, the doors off the closet. They threw clothes all over the room. Are they going to keep on searching forever? And once again she asked herself those questions that only have their answers in the end.

They began finding: spray paint pictures. One of them painted the walls with five-pointed stars and huge swastikas. And they laughed and laughed, and Sara managed to get a peek, she wanted to see, but the knuckles from a hand against her mouth changed her perspective.

Somebody's got to know. How did they get here, how. There were no clues, nothing. And my dreams? My crazy dreams. They've come, they're here. The men talk as if they're reading her mind. They say: Your little Hugo tried to get smart; he didn't give this address at the factory, so we went to see what we could find at mommy and daddy's house. And we did find something: we dug up the rent receipts to this place. Real clever, giving us the slip like that.

And the howling laughter. And the boxes that were opened. They piled newspapers and books on the table. They counted them. Just like cash.

The wall crumbles against the back of Sara's head, what are they after, what are they breaking, the whole house is falling apart, I can't breathe. They slung her to a chair, they slammed her down. Yes, now she opened her eyes completely and saw all of them, eight or ten, surrounding her. They searched, they found nothing.

And Hugo. Sara was sitting. They left her sitting there. They no longer hit her and they almost didn't insult her. She wanted to open her mouth, she wanted to say something. They suddenly became interested, they were all ears. What do they expect me to say?

Let's give it a try: Could you do me a favor? There's a plaid handkerchief hanging from the bedroom window. It's clean. Would you mind bringing it over to me?

A dark flavor leaked from her nose. They didn't believe her. A few of them looked over at the window; they could see the handkerchief but made no move to get it. The others: Let her go get it herself, but keep an eye on her, it could be a trap. Stick to her close. And she went to retrieve it, with several gun barrels right behind her.

Nothing exploded; they relaxed. It was over. The moment had passed, and now her fellow *compañeros** wouldn't come near the house.

Now she watched them as they wrote on an official-looking piece of paper, the arrest order, or something like it.

In a ditch. And what about me? If they killed you, why should they let me live? Arrest order: judgment. The huge fat one, who seems to be inside Sara's head, tells her right then and there: And now, baby, in just a minute, it's into the ditch next to your Hugo.

Anyway, as long as it's a shot, or two, it's no big deal. It's over quick. Hopefully right to the head. I wonder what you see, what shape, what color everything takes on, the air. Too bad. If all

---

*The term *compañeros* has a variety of meanings but, used here in the masculine or feminine plural, it has a decidedly political connotation, roughly equivalent to the notion of "comrades."

the stuff about the afterlife wasn't made up, just think how much you could see from there. Shit. They're going to kill me.

Ants, or dead animals, or mud, and Hugo. If at least they leave me in the same ditch. Maybe then I'd be able to see him just before they shot me. At the very least that. To see where the bullets went in. Where the blood came out.

She closed her eyes halfway. The men wrote, counted newspapers, jotted down notes.

What Sara sees: the bed to the left, the clothes scattered everywhere and dirty. The walls still dripping wet paint. Glasses shattered into thousands of pieces, the refrigerator completely cleaned out, food strewn all over the place. The box. They didn't open it. She had to tell them: the box.

She could tell by the sky that several hours had passed. The tree shook. No more loquats.

And the jacket. Hugo's best jacket worn by the skinny one, the one with the gash across his forehead, wearing the look of someone who just closed a major business deal. And the typewriter hanging from the fat one's hand. The fat one with the very same expression starting from his pupils, coloring the whites of his eyes.

Now what? They were taking her away.

She spoke: That box, that one you didn't open, leave it alone. I keep my sister's clothes in it. Where's your sister, you sorry-assed bitch? Fists against her back.

Dead. Years ago.

They dragged Sara out. They threw her into one of the three cars parked out front. Some of the cops went along with her, others stayed behind. Taking over everything, Sara thought.

Sometimes others decide for you. The more effort I put into staring at one point in the middle of the windshield, pretending to be off in some other world, the more the men figure that what I really want to do is keep my eye on the road, and they push my head between my legs. Shoes.

My black moccasins caked with dirt. Shabby. Through a hole in the right one I can see the joint of my big toe. What's that sticking out from underneath the front seat? A rifle butt. If the set-up was just a little easier, I could pull it out a little and really shake things up. If only. My hands are lashed behind me. If I had long flexible teeth I wouldn't even need to move: just a stretch, a tug on the trigger, and watch the shit fly. Just a canine. They wouldn't know what hit them. Sure, they'd work me over and spit me out. But who could deprive me of the satisfaction?

How stupid. My sister's clothes. I should have kept them hidden somewhere else. That's the last time I'll see them.

First my sister and now me. Nobody left around for my parents to screw with. Both daughters dead; it doesn't matter how. If I could just leave them a message with someone.

To keep a dead person's clothes as a reminder now seems a little odd to me. I used to open that box and study the shoelaces of her sneakers, the embroidering, the folds of her pale blue nightgown. And swallow the particles of skin still preserved in her things, pulling from me tears so complex, so obscene.

I hope there's not so much as a pair of panties left in my parents' house. So they can't keep anything of mine.

This is getting old. Where are they taking me? My neck hurts. Looks like they're stopping. The ones in front get out. You want anything from the store? Get me some Marlboros, says the one who's holding my head down, or maybe it's the other one. And get some candy for the sweetie. Hey baby, want some chocolate? and he jerks hair out. I wonder what they'd do if I told them what kind of candy I wanted? I'd better keep my mouth shut.

These two talk to each other. They talk about a cousin who's going to Europe. Europe just doesn't hold together for me. It bounces off the walls of my stomach, around in my head. I don't understand. I can't quite figure out the meaning of the word. Europe. It's something other than this. Europe. I wonder who that cousin is?

Here they come. The cigarettes hit me on the back.

The car began to move again. And Sara continued to ask herself questions. I'll find out soon enough. He lets go of my head to light the cigarette. I crane my neck and look: downtown. Then we're not going to the ditch? The guy doesn't quite strike the match: Put your head back down, cunt! Once again he places his hands around my neck but now he really loses his temper. She saw where we are, he shouts at the others. One of them spits in the backseat, spits at him. The one driving says it's no big deal, she'll find out soon enough anyway. He lets go of me and lights the cigarette.

Sara told herself almost without believing it that she was alive, or brought back to life, or asleep and in the middle of a storm. Not terribly sure, she chose instead to guess that she was alive, that in spite of the blows her bones were still intact; that her feet were frozen, but rather than a sign of death, this was just nerves, a case of plain and simple nerves. The blood had come to settle where it was needed: her stomach. She was no old corpse, they hadn't anointed her yet with perfume or oil. It was the fear, the uncertainty: her sweat.

Once again she wondered about Hugo. As the car pulled into the police station the driver told her that since she was so broken up, and considering that he was compassionate and didn't feed on hate like her and all the motherfuckers like her, he was going to inform her—and in a woman's voice he laughed, or vamped— that sweet Hugo was alive and at this very station, though he couldn't tell her for how long. He punctuated his speech by making his hand resound smack against Sara's face.

Others walk.

Adriana Receives Visitors

It didn't take too much of an effort for Sara to check into the new space that was assigned to her, since she was readily shown the way by a shove from behind; the ensuing slam of a door defined the whole situation for her. Amid the speed at which the events were unfolding, she made out the darkness of the place and a long bench on which she felt she could sit down. All of this while she became convinced of her total solitude, while she relied only on the walls and a wooden bench or two.

There were not a whole lot of alternatives. She ran her fingers around the edges of the bench and almost immediately resumed her bad habit of asking questions: she wanted to know what was going to happen as of that very moment. And as a result of that question, the voice of her mother echoed from within, that voice from when Sara was around five years old, when her mother, hysterically shaking her by the arm, would practically scream at her: Come on now, shut up, shut up, stop

asking questions, be patient, you'll find out soon enough! As to
why the bird in that painting had its severed head in one corner
and its body in the opposite one, as if the two parts didn't go
together, came the reply Shut your mouth! And a mild hatred
ran through her bones.

I want to know where I am. To see one of my *compañeros.*
With as many as these bastards haul in, is there no one here?
To talk, to hear a friendly voice. To have a fellow *compañera*
nearby. I want to pick up the noises, the silences. I want to wash
myself of all the uncertainty. This trembling and I just aren't
made for each other. There's a lighted room. Nobody told me
what I'm supposed to do. I can get closer by tiptoeing. I wonder
what's over there?

Sara rose unsteadily. She had a volcano in her stomach and
geysering up her throat, to her tongue, was a liquid acid, which
she pushed back down by swallowing hard.

When she reached the corridor area, she walked slowly,
pressing the side of her body against the right wall, thinking of
every possible way not to make noise. Until she heard a voice.
She stopped.

Until that moment she hadn't been able to deduce really anything. She didn't remember going down any stairs, but now,
looking up, there were some small windows with bars, through
which she could see several feet. That meant she was in a
basement.

The voice was faint, almost inaudible. Over the years she
would remember that phrase that ran through her head when
she heard it: You can separate the skull from the spinal column
of any bird. In spite of the weakness of the sound, Sara picked
up something in that voice: a dark overtone, powerful, which

planted in her mind the slotted lids of her mother screaming and shaking her.

I want to record that phrase. I can't get too far behind in the game. There's got to be some point of origin I can return to. This idea, that painting, and my anguish. I'm here and I have no idea where, halfway down a corridor through which I'm trying to pass and without the slightest idea of where it's taking me. This is no time for absurd thoughts. If I just move my fingers around, if I get them to warm up, this has to mean something. If I press the back of my head against this cold wall there must be a link connected with life or death, with my own sense of existence, with my interpretation of what I'm going through, with what I'm either willing or refusing to see. *The skull of a bird separated from its spinal column.*

She heard the voice again, and another one responding, conciliatory, trying to straighten out some unpleasant circumstance. Sara pressed her back flush against the wall and rested her head sidelong, squinting her eyes in the direction of the light. She felt flat, smooth. She fought off the tingling in her stomach brought on by the voices droning on about the meaning or lack of perspective in Egyptian art, and she associated the corridor with a half-open sarcophagus. Until finally she could no longer stand it. She took a step forward. She had to get there.

There were more voices, three, four, intermingled. The first one was always recognizable; it persisted with the certainty that it was set to go off on schedule. The voice gave her the impression of never stopping just to avoid slipping into an eternal silence. Sara took another step, still leaning against the wall, and another one, until she reached the end of the corridor. When she finally got to the source of the light, she poked her head in.

Women stretched out on metal, aqua-green beds. Twenty, thirty of them. Emaciated and sleeping or moaning. They lolled their arms over the sides of the beds, spoke to each other in whispery tones, turned their heads from side to side. Or they kept leaden stares fixed on the ceiling, their gazes invaded in some manner by fear.

That one saw me. They saw me. That craggy woman with a face that looked like a name full of *a*'s, but specially an Adriana; not Amalia or Amanda: Adriana. She sees my half head. She establishes herself, doesn't react. How come she doesn't say anything, why doesn't she point my head out to the rest of them? What does she find so strange that she looks at me with such a stupid expression? Am I doing something wrong? Is my face that beaten? I think it's about time I go in. To see who they are.

If they were *compañeras* of mine, if just one could tell me what the hell is going to happen here.

The woman flashed an empty smile, with an Adriana mouth, and threw a plaintive sound in her direction:

"Go on, come in. Or do you plan on standing there the whole time?"

All the others looked at her and followed the movement of her eyes and then discovered Sara's presence.

Sara still had that acid, which was now pouring into everything about her, soaking her completely through. She tried to preserve it as if it were the only thing that was her very own, private and personal among all the new changes. And as she observed the faces from her own parapet, she continued to discover her body a little more, since it seemed that the environment wasn't hostile. Some eyes exploded with curiosity, others looked at her as if it had been raining, as if it rained everyday.

And the old woman encouraged her to come closer, assuring her she was all out of options.

The woman is sure that there is only one direction to move, away from that metal threshold they stuck me through.

And Sara walked, her knees trembling, toward the old woman's bed. The others conceded a few "hellos" that Sara didn't return, at least not aloud.

"You're a *política,* aren't you?"

Sara said, "Yes."

"Not us. We're just regular ones. You all are the subversives. Why did they bring you here?"

"Surely to isolate her until she testifies in court," another one says.

The women were beginning to come to life, taking a certain interest in the new arrival who felt her blood circulating a little better, and she asked:

"There are political prisoners here? Where are they?"

"In the ward across the way from us. Come, have a seat."

Sara sat on the edge of the old woman's bed.

"Are they sick?" she asked, looking around at the others.

They all laughed, without answering. Until one of them, taken aback, remarked:

"Man, this look like a hospital or something? We could liven the place up a little. The radio. Hit the radio."

And immediately music filled the air, which Sara tried to take in but which definitely remained outside of her.

"And you, why are you all here in prison?"

"Everybody knows why. I'm a doctor, I run a childbirth clinic, the one they raided fifteen days ago. It was in all the papers. Did you read about it? Those two clean the clinic, that one is my partner, those three over there are nurses, and there are four or five others who happened to be there, clients, when the cops showed."

A third voice, smiling, urged the old woman to speak in the past tense.

"Clients? Patients," Sara objected.

"Clients. They were waiting for newborns."

"What did they charge you with?"

"Abortion and baby trafficking."

"When do you get out?"

"They say we're in for a long time. I don't really believe them, though. They want money. And what about you?"

"They found some papers on me."

"You're cooked then. You *políticas* are really cooked. We just cough up a few pesos. Maybe offer a couple of kids to the police station or court employees, those sterile bastards, and within a month we'll be up and running again. Hey, don't look at me in disgust, honey. Life's tough."

"I'm not disgusted. I just don't feel good. I'm worn out."

"Did they work you over much? They really let you all have it."

"My stomach feels like it's been thrashed."

"Get in bed. Look, that empty one over there is yours. Try to get some sleep. Let's see if we can't fix you up with something hot."

"They took my clothes. Books, my typewriter. Hugo's jacket. A couple of them brought me here while the others stayed behind loading up a car with all our things. Thieves."

"Lie down."

Sara sat up almost without moving and noticed two women

getting out of their beds. One brought water from the darkened area on the other side of the wall and another one placed a small pot on the burner. She heard two things at the same time: the question, so natural, a *Flaca,* how much sugar? and the other, the metallic noise of that first little door. Sara pricked up. She heard an "It's nothing, just the guard," directed at her uncertainties and striding in came the guard, short and slim, her head covered in blonde curls: The new one doesn't get undressed; they're going to take some pictures. And here are the aspirins that Adriana Benetti sent for.

Sara tried to figure out who was moving to that name, and the doctor with the cavernous voice boomed Thanks, and a young woman handed her the aspirins.

Adriana was almost like a queen in the basement:

"Guard, this girl is pretty banged up. Shouldn't she get to bed?"

"They take her pictures now and then she goes to bed." The guard disappeared down the dark corridor.

"Well then, come here and let's talk," Adriana called over to Sara once again. Someone handed the tea to her.

"And the rest of them, why are they here?" Sara asked.

"That little brunette bitch, instead of getting an abortion, waited until the baby was born and then she drowned it in a bucket of water. A neighbor turned her in. The one on the third bed from the back shot her husband three times, except she didn't finish the job. What I don't understand is how she has a husband, with that nose of hers. The fake blonde across the way there had a fight with her mother and whacked her over the head with a stick, breaking her skull open. And it goes on just like that, dear. To that beat. While you're in here you'll eventually find out about a lot of things. And those two that won't come over here, see them? They're prostitutes. They never fit in anywhere. They feel that the regulars like us are high class. We really make them sick. I can imagine what you must be feeling facing all of us. All the political ones are professionals and students, from rich families. Or almost all of them, right?"

"Not that many, fortunately. But you're a professional, aren't you?"

"Yeah, but by working my ass off. I come from the bottom. And now they've knocked us off our horses. My husband is also a doctor. You know what this does to our reputation? Whenever we get out of here those bastards are going to make us out to be pariahs. As if they were saints."

"Who?" with the tea stuck in her throat.

"All the other doctors."

They had turned off the radio and loud shrieks could be heard. Sara investigated and spotted two women arm in arm, singing at the top of their lungs in a prodigious effort to get the whole ward to pay attention to them. Adriana winced as if she had a bad attack of heartburn. She closed her eyes and with a shred of a voice said: "They're just awful. But they sing with so much conviction, tell me, how can you possibly get mad at them? Not even Gardel* was so sure of what he was doing."

And straining, they belted out an ungodly creation. Sara was rescued: they called her for pictures.

They placed her against the wall, front view, full body, left profile, right profile. She looked around for the other ward across the way and saw, yes, she saw some iron bars; nothing

---

*Carlos Gardel (1887–1935), world-famous Argentine tango singer.

more. She couldn't avoid the forms her anguish was slowly assuming. She passed back through the dark area between the two wards with a knot in her throat that dissolved when she saw the light and her ward mates. They reminded her that the bed was still waiting for her. Sara sat on the edge of Adriana's bed.

"I looked but I didn't see any of my *compañeras.*"

Adriana shot her a gimlet look.

"Get to bed. And stop asking questions. Be patient. You'll find out soon enough."

This old woman, so much solidarity before and now not even the time of day. She thinks she's royalty. My bones are getting cold. Once again, the image of that bird separated in two enters my mind.

Sara was walking toward her bed and heard Adriana order: "María, ask the guard for the iron. The ones across the way have it."

"At this hour?"

"Yes. At this hour. Tomorrow I have early visitors."

The daily routine. They get all dolled up for the visitors. With what motivation, I ask myself. They aren't going to let me see anyone, but hopefully they won't decide to stop me from seeing everything.

She went to bed. She looked around; she felt her stomach ache down to her feet. She wanted to let out a moan and tried to fall asleep. She stretched her arms out, away from the bed. She found herself staring at the ceiling: the synthesis of fear. The photos just taken, then the beating, then this hospital, or whatever it was. Everything bounced around inside, outside, and inside her mind.

She awoke when Adriana, iron in hand, roused her with a

surprising gentleness, made her get up, and took her to the bathroom where she locked them both in without a sound and, using a knife as a screwdriver, took the iron apart. It was the first time Sara had seen the inside of an iron. She marveled at how Adriana, with the fingers of a surgeon, extracted tiny pieces of paper that had been folded over several times, handing them to her. At how she then put the iron back together and left the bathroom, closing the door behind her.

Sara just sat there on the toilet. She opened the first of the papers and read:

Dear *compañera:*

We saw you when they took your pictures but we didn't show ourselves for fear you would get excited and wave at us, and the cops would be onto us . . .

Elsa

Sara swallowed a sigh; her muscles began to relax, and she even remembers that she closed her eyes for just an instant before reading on.

The shoes walk by themselves.

Sandals, Ernesto,
Tears, and Tea

To Graciela Maglie

"I could get half a cup of coffee with what I have." Sara checks her wallet.

"My treat. You haven't changed. How many years did you suck down in there anyway? Three and a half? You know I can't even tell? To see you alive, *flaca!* With all we've been through. And what we're still going through. Let me touch you—I know, I must seem nuts. But I'm touching you to believe it. We kept track of you. We found out about the basement, about Devoto. And to have you here now, less than two feet away . . . See my goose bumps? Here, look at this picture: my little girl, our third. We had her in order to have something new to hold onto. We just couldn't take it anymore. We still can't. Lia stays with me for reasons that make me want to weep. And as for me, I don't even want to tell you. So there we are: a real mess. But tell me about yourself. You all are the ones who've got to do the talking. You're just the same. Tell me how you've changed. No way; something must have been incubating inside of you. You'll show it eventually. I'm listening."

"I brought this for you to read."

"What is it?"

"Stuff written inside. I was able to save them. Poems."

"How did you get them out?"

"Just read them."

"What's wrong? Tell me. You don't talk as much as you used to."

Sara searches for words. She doesn't talk less than she used to.

"This is just a preview." Sara clenches her teeth, she tries to avoid stepping on the clothes and food that have all been thrown together on the floor.

The guards and monitors have just left, satisfied with the efficiency of the recently finished search. Each day they become a bit more proficient in the way they treat their little subversives. Now they withdraw to eat. The girls are once again back in the ward. And they try to turn it back to normal, and bras, pants, blouses, and panties fly from one end of the ward to the other. This one's yours, that one's Jimena's, that blue bra is mine.

Someone answers Sara: "Surely, it's just a preview." And her eyes must be almost closed. The rest of them don't feel any need to speak.

The space is infinite and enclosed. Everything is there, nothing needs to be brought in from the outside. Right there the juices are secreted, left to sit; the product is mixed and aged. You can well imagine there's some sort of witch, hunched over the cauldron of the daily, misty moods that are the inhabitants of that basement, manipulating the brew; this witch who's continually putting tweezers, nail clippings, and sickly, wizened finger bones to use. It all seems planned out in the upper regions, where a group of mysterious beings controls the effects of the witch's craft. But reality is far less delirious. And as for whatever walks over them, yes, the prisoners are kept in the basement; that much is true.

"We'll have to figure out a way to hide everything we possibly can. The next search will be fatal. Besides, I'm worried about my poems." Sara insists on talking. Nobody answers.

They recovered. A few days passed. They waited, they knew that changes were in store. During the first few months the ward was separated from the guard area by a tall, wide grating. In the dizzying advance toward perfectionism, they sealed off the ward with a sheet of metal that kept the prisoners buried inside for over a year. The welders arrived dressed as policemen, with huge blowtorches and 9 mm guns hanging from their belts. For a long time sparks were flying, though none shot off too far into the ward. The welding sparks were a strange, paradoxical form of light. None of the prisoners could keep from staring at the fireworks that came from the grating being fitted. There was a fascination, a felicity in that blue-orange madness. Many of them know that in some way this made up for the lack of sunlight, the persistence of those five or six fluorescent lights that over the course of months turned the skin of their faces and hands green.

They were walling them up inside the ward. They were burying them. But the sparks seemed fresh, from another dimension; they shot off, free of any guilt at all.

The women studied the movements of the cop-welders: doing their best (for the ones welding were observing too, consumed by curiosity to see what the true face of the terrorist really looked like) not to get emotional, not to shake.

A climate of various methods of suffocation was being prepped, just right so that the next search would hit the women spang on the back of the head.

But then something ensued, a kind of spin on the silence: a mass of sounds, immobilized and unable to circulate through the lack of space, began applying pressure against the walls. Nobody had screamed or talked. But the faint waves were composing sounds that couldn't quite be heard. And the dire need for space brought the women together. They busied themselves with finding space in the mattresses, pillows, in their clothes, in their own bodies, space that would preserve the treasures that kept them going: ballpoint refills, slips of paper, little books, a wristwatch or two, minus the band. They stashed everything and waited, on edge, until the next search. Which came.

The cry "Don't move, don't move, this is a search" from the guards struck against everything that was solid in the ward. They rushed in with the force of trained attack dogs. After an individual shakedown, they removed each one of the prisoners and proceeded to stick them a few at a time in the ward across the way, which was empty, which was kept empty until more people could be brought in off the streets of Rosario. They stayed behind with two of the inmates, Elsa and Sol, who were held accountable for everything the guards found and didn't like.

Unchecked and bosses of everything, they destroyed whatever they could get their hands on. They further reduced the space available to the inmates by closing off two cells and what was called the kitchen, the area where food was distributed and where books were usually kept.

From a stream of light leaking through the door of this

makeshift ward, the prisoners, during the wait, saw Elsa and Sol being dragged up the basement stairs by their hair. They saw them disappear.

Hours later everyone in the temp ward was returned to the regular one. Within a few minutes they were desperately screaming out for their missing *compañeras,* screaming about the general and detailed destruction of everything and the reduction of living space.

"Where are you?! Answer us," the screams alerted the entire police station. The two *compañeras* finally answered. They were now being held in the ward across the way, supposedly punished for resisting the closing off of the so-called kitchen. When the screams then changed to "Guards, bring back our *compañeras,*" the women all looked at one another and said: "The guards' faces are masked," just as they calculated the rapidly shrinking distance between the small windows of the basement and the police in charge of ripping out the screening, thrusting the launchers through the bars, and firing off the tear gas grenades.

Finding cover was nearly impossible amid the disorder and destruction, and the sparks from the two tear gas canisters happened to land on the mixture of kerosene and sugar that coated parts of the basement floor. A blanket thrown on top of the disaster by one or two *compañeras* wound up putting it out. Two voices were heard after the silence, voices of surprise and fear; one that said, "There's one less time we just died," which didn't get a response. The ones closest to Sara knew it was her. The ones who weren't near her figured it out. And another voice, absurdly disguised in a falsetto tone, chanced a joke, cracking: "How did we get into this screwy situation! Never did I imagine this could happen to me!" And this unleashed a blast of laughter that stretched across the ward and was eventually choked out with the gas. This was how they knew nobody was hurt or too shaken up.

In the darkness, crawling one by one so that their movements could not be detected from outside, crying, and scratching every inch of skin across their bodies, they reached the bathroom, where it was easier to breathe.

After a couple of hours, when they began to regain their composure, they decided, all of them herded in with a thick cloud of gas that was not going to dissipate any time soon, to put the ward gradually back into order. It was almost ten o'clock at night and someone suggested that some tea might not be half bad. They gave up that idea when they discovered the tea bags swimming in a bucket filled with detergent, bleach, and another strange substance that was best left unidentified.

All the lights in the basement were turned on from the guards' room so that now the prisoners were completely visible, their movements followed closely through the small windows from which they themselves could also see, though not nearly as easily, the heavily reinforced perimeter guard squad stroll by.

A few articles of clothing, a metal plate, a tin cup, and a spoon were left behind for each person. Cotton for menstruation, most of which was sopping wet and had to be wrung and left out to dry before it could be used. Toilet paper shredded by razor blades or scissors, and toothpaste, which the cops had gone to the trouble to empty, tube by tube, into nylon bags, to verify that the paste didn't hide anything that was prohibited. They confiscated all cigarette packs. From that day on, in order to smoke, the women had to roll their own; they themselves divvied up the tobacco and paper.

Many of the hiding places had been found out. Very few managed to survive with their contents intact. Three pairs of knitting needles made from the wood stripped from the beams of a few bunk beds fell out; so did a copy of *Teresa Batista cansada de guerra,** along with another large quantity of books too bulky to keep inside the nylon mattress. They took several notebooks with personal writings and book summaries, synopses and analyses of every kind, detailed diaries and poems, and among those things Sara's notebook, the one she worried so much about, the one that contained all her creative writing over the last two months.

And they found one of the two transistor radios, the only bridge between the street and the relativity of the underworld, not counting whatever news parents brought with them during the visits, which were continually pushed back by the prison officials, visits that more than anything filled the women in on the illnesses and disputes between cousins and old aunts.

That night the lights remained turned on as ordered by the station head, and the burning in their eyes wouldn't let them get to sleep.

A few days later only male visitors were allowed to come, a visit that lasted for less than half an hour. Each woman met with her father or brother in the secured area adjacent to the ward. Here was an opportunity to return summer clothes and shoes, because fall was just around the corner and anything they truly didn't need robbed them of the scarce space available in the basement. That was the final visit.

"Take these two pairs of sandals and this bag of blouses; it's going to get cold soon. I won't be needing them." Sara tried to stare hard at her father, to catch his eyes.

He left, after a search by the guard in charge, with the bag wedged under his arm, looking at the ground and not know-

*Or *Tereza Batista: Home from the Wars,* a novel by the Brazilian writer Jorge Amado.

ing when he would see his daughter again, or where, or under what conditions.

And then the trip back to the ward. Once again that anemic and deaf mass settled in, infiltrating every nook, every crack, every open space.

The hours pushed on and the day finally ended; and everyone slept. And in the morning, when it was possible for them to talk, Sara, sitting on the top bunk, told a number of inmates that what she had been doing during the two days before the search was to copy onto rolling papers, in an almost invisible handwriting, each one of her poems, open the lining of the straps of her summer sandals, and tuck the pieces of paper inside, and then reattach the lining to the leather.

"There. So I talked."

"So you talked! And after that, what's there left to say? Silence."

"No."

"Yes; you'll see."

"No."

"Yes. Keeping quiet. You and me. Both of us."

"Not me."

"You too. Just like everyone else. You aren't free; don't fool yourself."

"I'd never fool myself."

"So why don't you just give me those poems and hurry along, go have lunch at home. Come on now, be a good girl. I'll call you Thursday after I give them a read. I love you lots. Let me touch you again. We love you like this, alive. You're alive—you are alive, aren't you? Very much alive indeed. What's with that look? Well, aren't you alive? That's all I mean. That you're not dead. That's all. Well, whatever urges you get to enjoy life, fine. We'll talk soon. I'll give you a call on Thursday. OK?"

"No."

"Why *no?* Everything is no. Your old lady used to call you 'Why.' Why go to the store. Why walk straight ahead. Do you remember that? Because you were so inquisitive. Can't I call you on Thursday?"

"You can call me, but a good girl—uh-uh."

"Alrighty; anything you say. I'll give you back your poems (now you're going to say yes, I swear you will) and treat you to two scoops of ice cream. OK?"

"No."

"No?"

"Three scoops."

"Not another word. Or else I lose."

Ernesto smothers Sara with kisses, noisy kisses on the nose. He pushes her out toward the street, they leave the coffee shop together, they part at the corner. Sara watches Ernesto walking off and notices that he has a limp. He drags one leg, the right one, as though his shoe were filled with stones. That's new, Sara doesn't remember it. Sara asked herself: I wonder what kind of thrashing he got on that side over the last five years. And she answers herself: Yeah, probably a thrashing for being too clumsy. He might have tripped on a loose sidewalk tile, he might have broken his kneecap, maybe they set it improperly.

She still watches him. Ernesto must sense it, because from a half block away he turns around and looks for Sara, and now he spots her. He walks toward her. He reaches her. Once again, separated by a few inches, they look at each other. Sara had gone from concentrating on his right leg, the lame one, to his shoulders. She doesn't really know why. Ernesto stops on Sara's crinkled brow, her darkened eyes. And he says: you're so screwed in the head. He repeats:

"You're screwed in the head. You don't have any right."

"I didn't make a sound."

"Shut up."

"What did I say?"

"It's what you thought. That's what interests me, not what you said."

"OK . . . what was I thinking?"

"You had doubts. You have no right."

"If the shoe fits . . . "

"Jerk."

"All right. What happened to you then?"

"When they took my sister we all got it. They broke my leg while they were beating the crap out of me." He adds: "Yeah, you really pass yourself off as the heroic one. You saved your poems! The ones that will determine the destiny of mankind in the next century."

They are standing very close to the curb. A car goes by, they feel the air whip across their thighs.

"Why don't you come and eat with me over at my folks'?" Sara tries to pay attention to the car as it moves away. Its red top.

"Because you don't deserve it. I'll call you Thursday. And during the next few days until we see each other again, try, just try to make an effort and imagine the other reality." He smiles gently. "The one you didn't have to live. That other one that others lived. You and your crazy imagination. Here's my reality, for example: the *milicos* broke my leg when they raided my house looking for my sister and I recovered from that. Years later I allowed myself the luxury of playing in a soccer game and broke my kneecap, and they set it wrong. In a month I'm going to have surgery again. Whether you like it or not." Defiantly. Ernesto clenches his jaw, squints, and sweeps his gaze across Sara's face, who observes him, curiously. He lowers his eyes and doesn't look up at her again. He finishes with a "Thursday," and limps off.

Some feet dance. Pirouette.

Sara, Elsa, Marco, and the Dance of Great Sadness

Sara, how do your legs walk, what are you feeling out with the tips of your feet, your toes, what do your knees perceive with each bend? What images pooling in the back chambers of your brain, in the shifting shapes of your perceptions, are transforming you? What pulls you out of the space of your own magnitudes, Sara, and what puts you back within your own giving limits? What is it that breaks down your bent for nostalgia, mixing you in with other ways, new ones for you, of fighting to recover your emotions. *To live,* comes out of your mouth, *You have to live this because it's a part of existence.* And aside from your body that is you and your mind that takes you down the tortuous roads, swerving to avoid obstacles for you, who knows what you're looking to prove? Looking to justify. Looking to rationalize.

If only you had always been so morally rigorous. If ever since you can remember, you've felt deep down that your friends' husbands are statues. Not men. Oh, Sara. Oh, don't force me to look at you askance.

To what existence are you referring? What do you picture as the phonemes tumble out of the hollows of your mouth, one at a time, and begin appearing like rivers on a map only to reshape themselves right before your very eyes in that same final format: *existence*. Sara, honey, that word has had it. In reality—you of all people should know this—existence consists of searching for, of finding words that are more and more original, that burst with meaning, words that give us a chance to withstand the tedium. So come on. Let's get to work. It's virgin territory, and what you so cheekily call existence is really something greedy for meaning.

And watch out for greed. If you don't learn to give it the proper nourishment, it'll eat you up.

Then maybe Marco isn't a statue, even though he is Elsa's husband. You should ask yourself why that is. Can't you see that his eyes are closed? He's in a deep sleep. Marco sleeps the sleep of a husband. Of a friend's husband. Friend: not the one you might have bumped into yesterday on the way to the market, the one who asked you the price of the lettuce because it wasn't clearly marked on the shelf. No, no, Sara. No. Those other women. You and I are those women too. Repeatedly shown by life's circumstances—which are not abstractions—that the world needs people willing to put forth their bodies, their time, their eternal existence, to try to strengthen human life. Those women. Who defined their enemy. Who concentrated on the fight. Women whom that enemy, having won the battle, physically holds in its grip. Along with you. Women who shared with you, four at a time, a cell meant for only one. Those friends,

Sara. Ones who day after day exchanged frightened looks with you. Looks of understanding. Looks of farewell in the face of imminent death.

Those friends, Sara.

Elsa. The one who oiled your joints, rusted from putting your strong defense mechanisms to use at any unusual event, risky, life-saving, coming from inside an iron. The one who guided you through the emotional labyrinth that the ward of political prisoners embodied for you in that moment, in that basement. Just what are you trying to do, Sara? How come her husband, the one who waited up for her, who supported her, who raised their son, is *not* a statue to you? Why is it that your alleged principles, your concepts of morality and respect, your notions of love and unselfishness collapsed just like that, sluicing away the remains of the disaster down the drain.

(SARA AND MARCO'S VERSION)

"I can't tell you how happy I am to have you here, Sara."

"Yes . . . Well, I believe this is what you want, more or less. Let's see what you think."

"It's poetic. But it's lacking."

"Some polish, right?"

"No. I'd say a bit of happiness, that's what's lacking."

"A bit of happiness? Is that what's lacking? I can't believe I'm hearing this. *You're* saying that to me? Can't you see the expression on your face? You look dead. Don't you even see that?"

"Just be a little patient with me, please. I too was once 'a happy man.'"

Patience. For Sara patience is a sure ticket to hell. Wait. Wait for what? Standing around makes her want to cry. And the words of certain human beings: Wait, Be patient, Everything comes—while this is on the way, go and do something else. Those words, so intent on planning out life in such a way as to obtain the most advantages and the most effective long-term benefits, overwhelm her. Sara is overwhelmed. She has one of those fears that settles into some corner of her lymphatic system like a parasite, eating up what few defenses she tries to preserve, secretly, for an emergency.

Marco looks at her. He looks her right in the eye. Sara touches Marco's hand, the one resting on the desk. Very lightly.

"Marco, listen to me. I'm scared. My husband is in prison and I love him. I really do love him. But I think I'm falling for you."

Sara knows these words are dictated by that portion of stupidity that at least twice a week, coming from who knows where, makes its way through one of her openings and dominates her on the inside. And she can't stop talking: "And I love Elsa. I can't figure out what's wrong with me. She's my friend, and I get the feeling that whatever belongs to her is also my property, just because she's my friend. Marco, I didn't want this to happen. I really didn't. I know I don't have the right to feel this way, or even to tell you this."

"Now you listen to me. And listen good: First, I'm not anybody's property. Second, yes, you have the right. Everybody has the right. I have the right."

A kind of acidity inside Sara finds her tongue: "I don't mean to be so blunt, but I wonder what your opinion would be if Elsa came out of nowhere with the story that she was in love with someone else."

"I'm married to her, but that doesn't mean she belongs to me."

"And you, of course, don't belong to her, which you think gives you the freedom to cheat on her, right?"

A kind of pain inside Marco finds his hand. He whacks the ballpoint pen against the desk, again and again, out of control. The pain spreads to his tongue: "What about you, huh? Seems to me that after four years of sharing almost everything with your cell mates you ended up kind of getting used to it. That's great!"

"Are you saying that all of this is my fault?"

"What do you mean by *this?*"

"I mean *this.*"

"*This* what? I don't know what you're getting at. I can't see a thing."

"Come on Marco, don't be silly. I guess I don't even know what I'm saying. I shouldn't say anything. I shouldn't even be here."

"Sara, do me a favor. Sit down. Sit down for just a minute."

"Fine. Happy now? Look, I'm feeling pretty vulnerable at this moment in my life. There's something about you that I can't exactly say what it is I like, but it makes me feel really close to you. I don't know what it is. But I do want to help you with your work here, in this bogus position you made just for me, though I know perfectly well you don't need me. At the same time, I can't stop coming here."

"You can't stop coming *or* talking, Sara."

And it's true: "I can't say no. I have to come and see you and I know it's not fair. Elsa's my friend. She's going to hate me. She's going to hate me. This is crazy. Completely crazy."

"I don't need to get into how I feel about you. At least not in words."

The same hand that before was smashing the pen against the desk now approaches Sara's hand and takes it, lightly tracing over it. Marco needs all kinds of tenderness and he softens: "If you're telling me these things it must be because you know perfectly well that you're very important to me. We're going to have to talk about that. Then we'll see what happens next. It's hard for me to be close to you, and at the same time force myself to keep my distance. It looks like we're in the same boat . . . Your being here really does help me out, just being close to me everyday. I need to get away from all the anguish in my recent past. I need someone like you."

"I can't believe I'm hearing this."

"Just tell me what you need. I'll do whatever is necessary to get it for you."

"I need for you to be just a little bit happy. *Now*."

Sara is being wracked, invaded, by that cold. Her muscles, the edges of her eyelids. And she pulls back. Sara suddenly pulls back, she withdraws her hand and walks over to neutral ground: "I have two things to tell you. The first thing is that I'm going to La Plata. I got permission to leave Rosario for twenty-four hours, so I'm going to visit Hugo in jail. I have to leave on Thursday. The other thing is that I'm sure I'm being tailed. I just want you to know so you can make a decision about my working here."

"Let me go with you. I have a lot of experience handling those kinds of procedures."

"Don't even think about it. One thing, though: if I'm not back on the three o'clock bus on Friday, call the two phone numbers I'm going to give you. And I'm serious when I tell you

to think long and hard about whether I should continue working here. Now you have more than one reason to change your
mind."

"Sara, please, just shut up."

Marco turns his head toward the closed office door, thinking
he had sensed some sort of vibration. Yes, the door opens, and
it's Elsa. It's Elsa, who walks in resolute, smiling.

"And now . . . the power of the gaze!" She acts like a robot.
She stands in front of Marco and Sara, all stiff, her eyes fixed on
Sara. She waits for her reaction. But she can't hold back: "I decided to get rid of my glasses. I got contact lenses. The 'soft
ones.'"

Sara feels the trembling in her knees, but she rises from the
chair and stands. They each plant firm kisses on the other's
cheek. Sara carefully studies Elsa's eyes, now visible and pleas-
ant, and despite the partial breaking up of the air around the
three of them she can still hear, and she hears Elsa—wearing a
very lucid expression that covers her whole face and spreads to
her whole body—finish what she was saying: "Now I can see
everything so clearly. So very clearly!"

(SARA AND MARCO'S VERSION,
A FEW DAYS LATER)

Sara walks down the hallway and hears classical music. But she
knows that an ad agency with young people needs a constant fix
of Peter Frampton, the Beatles, Creedence. In order to survive.
Her shoulder bag weighs her down. She walks in. No one in
the office. But Marco's cigarettes, his lighter, glasses, address
book, everything is there. He must be close. Close. Sara senses

something. A movement on the hardwood floor. She turns around. Marco. He's there. He observes her, far too sternly. And just in case there's something in his stern look she doesn't want to uncover, something she doesn't want to hear from him, she beats him to the punch: "The bus was late."

"How's your husband?"

"So so . . . He was hoping to be out by Christmas."

"I had a long conversation with Elsa last night."

Marco turns and turns and turns the lighter over in his hand. His words are like chewing gum. Sara doesn't want to listen.

"What about?"

"Well . . . I didn't mention the word *divorce* but . . . "

"Come again?"

"I . . . we . . . I mean, I was trying to make her understand that things are not forever."

"Why?"

"Why? Because I love *you*. That's why."

"You didn't tell *her* that, did you?"

"No, Sara. Your name wasn't brought up. But . . . "

Sara is afraid. She doesn't want to listen. Marco doesn't want to speak. He's afraid. But he goes on: " . . . but she seems to know something. I don't know exactly what."

Sara becomes impatient. She doesn't want this. She doesn't want it.

"What else?"

"Don't be afraid, Sara."

"I'm not afraid. I'm worried. What else would I be?"

"Worried about what? if I may ask."

"Elsa is hurting."

"Most likely. But it's not your fault. Nor mine."

Sara's legs itch. She stands up. The bottoms of her feet are tingling. She walks, walks in circles, making herself dizzy, making Marco dizzy, cracking up the air, kicking up the piles of paper on the desk.

"Marco, listen. Please, listen to me. We, being the creatures we are, have certain limits. Our feelings and thoughts are definitely limited. And that really frightens me."

"Who's this we?"

"You and I. Do you want to know what I feel right now? I want to go back to prison. I miss my friends. I feel guilty. They should be free, all of them. And sometimes I think I don't deserve this freedom I have. Look at what I'm doing. I'm celebrating my freedom by putting you in the position of cheating on your wife. You didn't do it when she was in jail. But you do it now, when she's free. This is all so ridiculous."

Her compulsion won't allow her to stop; she walks, opens and closes her fists: "You know what? I need to feel free. I can't live this way."

"You just said you wanted to go back to prison."

"Well, this is not the kind of freedom I had in mind."

Marco follows her with his eyes; he is irritated: "I know what you mean. You need a different kind of freedom. Now I get it. You seem to know a lot about that word: *freedom.* And tell me something, did it ever occur to you to look it up in the dictionary?"

"No. Never."

Defiant Marco. Unbudging. Well, maybe not so unbudging: "OK, then just settle down and listen. Sit."

He watches Sara comply, stop pacing in circles. "I have. This morning. That word has a lot to do with me, too. Don't you think?"

"And so, what does freedom mean in your dictionary?"

"It's the ability to act, to proceed . . . " Marco stands, walks slowly, though not in circles, just straight, toward the door, and before he leaves the room he shoots Sara a meaningful look, and he finishes: " . . . or not to act."

Some feet rest.

(SARA AND ELSA'S VERSION)

"I wish this kitchen had more space."

"Let me wash the dishes, Elsa."

"No. I'll wash, you dry."

"Elsa, who tells you about their dreams now?"

"In this house, Sara, the only one who dreams is my son. And he still has nightmares. Don't be so surprised. You too must be having bad dreams. Am I right?"

"Elsa, I . . . "

"Sara, please, don't say anything. All you have to do is think."

"I think all the time, I think and cry, my head is going to explode. I love you, and you know that."

"No. I don't know that."

"Please."

"Please, please. Please what? Don't you see what you're doing? Do I have to tell you what you're doing to me, to my son, to my life?"

"Let me tell you about my feelings."

"Your feelings? I can't believe this. Your feelings. Just what feelings are you talking about?"

"My feelings for you, for . . . "

"No, Sara, no! I know what you want. You want me to listen to everything you can possibly think of to say about your feelings for my husband. That's what you want. You want me to be patient. To understand."

"I want you to know I love you."

"Oh sure, you *love* me. That's just what I was thinking . . . Thanks, Sara, now my life is so complete. Without your love I'd die. Do you know what I think? Did my opinions ever really matter to you? I'm going to tell you what I think. You're out of your mind. If this is what a few years in jail did to you, then what kind of militant were you? What kind of person are you? And tell me, what about your husband? *I love you, Hugo . . . I want you to know I love you . . . "*

"Elsa, listen, you're very upset and you have a right to be. But can I ask something of you?"

"Of course, Sara. I'm always at your service. Do you want my son Lucas, too?"

"I want a chance to have a conversation somewhere else. Away from your house."

"What's wrong with the kitchen in my house, huh? You feel weak in enemy territory, right? No problem, Sara. No problem. Give me a ring, sweetie, and we'll set a time. Now get out of my house. Right now!"

And the plate that Elsa is about to hand Sara to dry breaks against the faucet. It breaks, it shatters, and the pieces scatter to the floor. Because Elsa wants it that way.

That same night Sara waits for Elsa at a corner. Confused.

Afraid. All set to explain, even against Elsa's wishes. If she shows up. She has dressed attractively, made up her eyes a bit. And yes, Elsa's approaching. Wearing the pants that look best on her, with that black sweater that makes her taller, more stylish, more noble. She's made up her eyes, done her lips. Sara searches out Elsa's eyes. Elsa has found an attitude to hide behind today, a conduct for these circumstances: defiant, yes that's it, defiant. They walk together, without acknowledging each other, but they walk side by side. Their elbows rubbing together. They make use of the slow pace, take advantage of it, overuse it, until Elsa finally confronts her: "You don't think after all this we can still be friends, do you?"

"I can't believe you're willing to forget all those years of friendship."

"How could you say that, Sara? How can you twist things around to the point of accusing me of something you started? How could you? This is your madness, not mine."

"I'm not accusing you of anything, I'm only appealing to your levelheadedness."

"So, I'm just supposed to let my best friend steal my husband away from me and not say anything about it? And then on top of that, I'm supposed to resolve the huge mess she's gotten us into just because I refuse to stick out my head so she can chop it off. I'm supposed to be sensitive, let her decapitate me, and be happy that my friend is having fun playing basketball with my head. That's just great."

"Happiness . . . Elsa, what are you talking about? How the hell can you even bring up that word?"

The plants, the trees at night. The plaza they're passing through. The bench they discover among the overgrown weeds.

They sit. Sara tries to make herself comfortable, props one foot up on the bench, studies the tip of her shoe, watches Elsa strike a formal pose, callous, looks again at the tip of her shoe, and once again it is Elsa who begins to speak: "Well, it would seem you're looking for something. If it's not that, that wonderful happiness, I ask myself what it is you find so attractive? An attraction that blinds you to the point of destroying my family, your life, Hugo's life. What are you so desperate for? . . . a man? Couldn't you find one somewhere else? Come on, Sara, please. You don't need a man. That's not your style. You're the kind of woman who handles life much better without a man getting in your way all the time. I know you. You need peace and quiet in order to write. That's what you should try to find."

"It's true, Elsa. I'm not desperate for a man. But I can't write either. I mean, I'm always working on something. Nothing serious though. I can't. I've got other things on my mind as of late."

"I can very well imagine."

"Elsa, no . . . I don't know . . . Look, I walk the streets, sleep, hang out with friends, shop, think, talk to people, go and sign in at the police station—I've got my routine, my goddamned routine. I'm supposed to be alive, I'm supposed to be free. But that's not how I feel. Do you want to know how I feel? By any chance do you have any interest in my feelings?"

"If you insist . . . "

"I feel like I'm sitting in a movie audience. Each little action, each word, isn't coming from me. I'm not the protagonist. I sit in a coffee shop and from the window I observe all the people walking, running to catch the bus, missing it, I see them talking to others, waving their hands around, I don't know, I see them living. I guess that's what they're doing. But it's like I'm so far removed from that. I'm in the middle of all that movement, but emotionally I just don't take part. It's like sitting there watching a movie. And not just any movie, but a really insipid one . . . Ever since I was released, I feel like a prisoner more than ever. In prison with everyone who hasn't been released yet. And I can't help but feel guilty for enjoying a freedom that doesn't just belong to me, but to all of us."

"You don't seem to be enjoying it at all . . . "

"Of course I'm not."

"The whims of the military aren't your fault."

"I know that, Elsa. But it's not the rational part that isn't working right. The problem is that objectivity just isn't working for me. I'm always imagining, imagining so many things. And I have that windmill turning in the pit of my stomach. Everything that goes on around me makes the windmill move and it exasperates me, it churns my insides. And my emotions are so strong, like explosions that make me flinch as I try to analyze myself, when I try to understand this life of 'freedom' we now have. They blindside me. They paralyze me. On the outside I have the involuntary reactions of an observer. I'm constantly fighting to put my feet on the ground, Elsa. And it's so hard to do. I'm not sure I can see what I do, or hear what I say. It's like I'm a kind of jigsaw puzzle I have to put back together every day just to recognize myself. So many things have changed over the past few years. There's been so much madness and so much horror. I guess I'm confused, Elsa. But it's not fair. None of this is fair. You've got to see it, acknowledge it, and leave the mental masturbation for a more appropriate time."

"About the guilt, I feel the same way. But not about the rest.

Maybe the difference is that when I was set free I had to confront very concrete and real problems: Lucas, Marco, my mother. You don't have those responsibilities. Hugo's in jail, you're alone. It *is* possible, I guess. At any rate, though, I still can't understand why you're so desperate."

"I told you I'm not. Not at all, Elsa."

"I think you are. To have reached the state you're in, you must have a big problem. And it's not that you're desperate for a man. It's not that at all. It's a desperation to feel alive. To confirm that you're still the same Sara. That they didn't destroy you. The brilliant, the generous, the courageous Sara, the writer with so much promise. The one in prison who always wore her best face. All the wonderful and complex ingredients she was made of. The one I'll never forget. The one who's now part of my past."

"Don't say that, Elsa, please. We, you and I, we both know so much about life. So much. Please. None of this happened because I wanted it to."

"Oh sure, *I* wanted it to happen."

"I can see you don't want to talk anymore, Elsa."

"I already told you—you expect me to go easy on you. You expect me to listen and accept anything you say, but you don't care about what goes on inside of me. You want me to justify your actions. That's impossible, Sara. It's precisely because we know so much that we have to understand. I need to end our friendship so you can understand, Sara, that the world is not all yours."

"Elsa, look at me, please. I understand. I'm not saying I'm as good as gold. I admit I made a mistake. But you're acting like this is the end of everything. You should remember all those times when we were so close to death. Listen, I don't want to give you the impression I'm just throwing words around. Even though this isn't the best situation for you, Elsa, I would like for you to remember the way we supported each other during all those nightmarish years, which aren't over yet. Maybe if you look back you'll understand that all of this is part of the same big picture. I love you. You are my friend. You, Cristina, and Ana María."

"You should have remembered that a lot sooner, Sara. I'm the one being affected by all of this. I lose my husband and my friend."

"You're not losing me."

"Sara, how can you expect me to accept that?"

"I don't expect you to accept anything. But I am appealing to your greatness of spirit. To your integrity. I'm trying to put your honesty and your strength to use because I can't appeal to mine. What I mean is that it doesn't matter whom these qualities belong to. In reality they belong to life, to this existence."

"Ah yes, of course. When those attributes are yours you want the entire world to know. But when they're mine, they're a part of life, or any other abstraction you can come up with."

"What I want to do, Elsa, even though this may sound strange, is to ask you, and I hope you understand me . . . I don't know, I'd like to borrow some of that good, natural predisposition of yours so I can put myself back together, so I can return to the way I once was. Do you think that would help me see what's going on in my life more clearly?"

"Wait a minute . . . Let me get this straight: you're asking *me* to help you?"

"Yes. I'm asking you for help."

"Well . . . yes, of course I can help you, if you're willing to do whatever I ask of you. For starters, let me give you a piece of advice. In order to correct nearsightedness, there's nothing that works better than 'the soft ones.' And let me tell you, if you wear the soft lenses, there isn't a thing that'll get past you, dear."

Sara is fashioned from a strange material. She doesn't know the answers. Each letter out of her mouth is like a pin jabbing Elsa's brain. And they make a hissing sound, which is the squirt of citric acid given off by the beating heart of the dear woman sitting next to her. By the beat of Elsa's bones. Sara doesn't find the answers. Elsa makes use of the emptiness of sound: "Let's see . . . why don't we recap what you're asking of me. First let's go over what you've got left: (1) Marco, (2) my friend-ship, (3) and most likely . . . "

"No."

"What do you mean, No?"

"I'm the one with nothing left."

"Excuse me, I don't quite get the deal you're trying to cut here."

"I don't want Marco."

"You're in love with him. Didn't you say that?"

"No. Well, yes, but my love for him doesn't interest me as much as our friendship does."

"But my dear, he's in love with you . . . And now you're going to leave him? You don't even care about *his* feelings?"

"I care much more about yours."

Elsa spreads an ostensible calm through the smoke-black air, her legs stretch inside the tight jeans to decide on her departure, and they rouse the darkness. Her neck, her chest, and her two round, ample forms lift to the rhythm of her legs, which stir the very meaning of the night: "Being the brilliant person you are, I'm sure you'll understand it's hard for me to believe you."

Sara has completely lost her ability to pick and choose. There are no more words worth the effort of stringing together and pronouncing. Any idea transferred to sound would make the particles that fill the air snake to the rhythm of Elsa's firm steps. Elsa, who is no longer there, who has left Sara watching her disappear and pushing down her throat the sick with which she savors her last meal.

Some feet walk.

(CRISTINA, SARA, AND MARCO'S VERSION)

Cristina's pores are open, stimulated by some chemical mixture floating in the atmosphere that fills the car. The mixture now intensifies and tries to fill the holes in her skin. But without any success: too thick for her skin to accept. She speaks. She speaks for Marco, who is relieved by the story. She speaks for Sara, who is relieved by the story because it allows her to laugh. Because it gives her a chance to imagine the prison she was in. Forget the prison she's in now. In between every letter out of her mouth, Cristina is alert to the pressure of this different air trying to penetrate her, and she feels the vibration of her skin when it rejects it. Marco drives his car, which takes Cristina and Sara home at the end of the day. Cristina is sitting in the front seat, fidgety, upset. Sara is practically coiled up in the back, listening, recognizing the words.

"And then I ask her, 'What are your poems about anyway,

protest?' And she answers, 'They're about whatever comes out of me.' She hated me. I swear to God Sara hated me. Her writing was so important to her, and I was making fun of her as a writer. Poor Sara."

They laugh. They all need to laugh. A kind of suction sound makes Marco turn his head around. And he looks at Sara. He looks at her. Cristina feels the pressure against her skin again. And the rejection. And then there is a silence. Each silence moving around in their own windpipes, maybe.

And the car, more or less guided by the instincts of its occupants, stops in front of the house where Cristina is renting a room. Cristina gets out of the car, shuts the front door, motions her hand as if to wave, to say good-bye, good-bye to something, she's saying good-bye to more than her friend Sara until they see each other the next day, and to the husband of her friend. Before turning from the car and going inside she slows her entire body to a stop and faces Sara through the rear window, looking at her with the same intensity as that pressure that affected her in the car, that pressure that seems to have gotten out of the car with her, ready to accompany her to bed. And Sara turns toward her. Her eyes meet Cristina's, but Cristina's eyes are like tree branches. What's wrong? Is it the window playing tricks with the distortions? Cristina's gaze is like two branches sticking right through Sara's eyeballs, pushing, plunging, crushing them against the back of her head.

The car begins to move again, and until Sara stops looking at Cristina, who's still standing at the sidewalk, in the distance, paralyzed, and with her eyes still fixed in Sara's direction, she can't turn her head around, she can't come back to herself, she can't summon up the strength to fight off the ache in her stomach that's beginning to make her feel like a caged animal. And Marco's voice: "When do I get to read your poems?"

And Sara: "I don't know. I'm working on some short stories now. Well, I'm always working on some nonsense." Trying. Trying to mask her discomfort.

The car slows down. And stops.

"Elsa told me that the only thing that kept her from going crazy inside was what you call your 'nonsense.'"

And Sara, despite the pain, perks up. She sits up, rests her arms on the back of the front seat: "That's what she tells you about me?"

Marco is so close to her. His nose, eyelids, so close. And he looks at her so seriously. For such a long time that Sara absorbs and reflects the same seriousness: "Do you want me to leave the agency?"

Marco stops looking at her. He lightens: "No."

He looks at her again, stretches his hand out to caress her head, but Sara has already opened the door to get out of the car. He stops her. He grabs her by the arm and reels her back in. He pulls her toward him, anxiously, with that kind of desperation that can be a gift for those who choose to stay alive, and a suicidal push for those who can't handle loss. He kisses her on the lips, and Sara answers with an "Elsa," and he kisses her on the forehead, and Sara answers with another "Elsa," and he kisses her on the cheek, and Sara repeats "Elsa," and he kisses her again on the lips, and Sara responds to one or two of the kisses and repeats over and over "Elsa, Elsa, Elsa, Elsa."

And little by little she slips loose, slides away, flees from Marco's kisses. She gets out of the car. And from outside, poking her head through the window, her eyes uneasy, fearful, like she's seen a tornado, she parts her teeth halfway and an air current from within pushes out words: "Even though Elsa's decision to end our friendship is irrevocable, she'll always be my friend. See you tomorrow at work."

And he: "What time do you have to report to the command post tomorrow?"

And Sara: "At 10 A.M. And I'm going by myself."

And the movement of the air mass that swings back and forth between them can almost be seen, they themselves can see it, entering and leaving the car through the window, varying in temperature, slowly at times, at times faster.

(ELSA AND MARCO'S VERSION,
THAT SAME NIGHT)

Elsa feels: eyes closed; the only way to understand, to individualize each event, even the unknown ones, the ones that can be sensed. Closed. The only way to forget about the existence of this carpeted floor on which I'm sitting, the recliner that I rest my head on, the front door that faces me and that I really wish would open. Open.

These jeans are tight. More than I'd like. But they look good on me. Something snaps, a part of my body turns to sleaze when I put them on. At the precise moment when I try to pull them up. When the waist and the zipper scratch my legs with the last few tugs. When I've just about got it. Something sleazy, something secretly moves around, grows warmer. It changes. It's a place in me I have no access to. Who knows? In the end, when the act has been consummated and I look into the mirror, it's easier for me to get out of my head the images from a dream I had, one in which hundreds of shopping carts, each one carrying the corpse of a newborn child, have filled this street, down the whole block, for a month now. And I can't. I don't want to open the door. That fear. That fear, that's like blue. Flat and smooth. No stripes, dots, or bumps. Acetic, with that icy light from who knows what winter from who knows what corner of the world. Somebody else should open it. From the outside. Someone who by turning the key will distract me, invade me with their presence, pick me up from where I am like a piece of furniture and set me back down in the dimension of reality. Not the reality that is. The one I want. After all, we are few in this world, we human beings. And in that small group, closer and tighter than we imagine, there must be someone who can see me, feel me as I exist, recognize my rhythms, relate them to their own. There's got to be someone. It can't be that I'm that far from feeling human.

Elsa listens: the key. Turning. And she opens her eyes. But before the door opens, she closes them again. Surely he took Sara and Cristina home. And now he's returning. To what? He walks toward me. He's standing in front of me. He's going to speak. Elsa opens her eyes. And they study each other. Elsa, from her spot on the floor; he standing in front of her, still, grave.

"Where is Lucas?"

"He's sleeping."

"Were you asleep, too?"

"Kind of."

"Were you waiting for me?"

And Elsa's acid-tipped reply: "No. I was waiting for my lover."

And Marco's acid-tipped reply: "Elsa, listen good: I have too many things to think about, too many problems to resolve. And I'm not in the mood to fight. So, please . . . "

And he wants to disappear. He walks toward the bedroom. Elsa bends her knees, plants her feet on the carpet, rocks on her heels for a second, then stands up and walks behind him.

Once in the bedroom Marco pulls off his sweater and Elsa sits on her side of the bed. She leans back against the pillow, folds her legs, hugs her knees. She looks at Marco. She explains: "Nor am I. But I think we need to talk."

Marco sits on his side of the bed, holding the sweater in his hand. "Now what?"

"Are you sure you don't love me anymore?"

"Did I say that?"

"In effect."

And Marco's weariness: "Let's see, what did I say?"

"For the last week you've been trying to convince me, in one way or another, that nothing is forever. And I need to know exactly what's going on between you and Sara."

"Nothing's going on."

Elsa's impatience: "Marco, please . . . "

"What do you think is going on? What did you tell her?"

"What, she didn't tell you everything we talked about, did she?"

"No. To be honest, I don't think she told me everything."

"Are you saying you don't really trust her, Marco?"

"It's not that. What I can see is that you *girls* will go to the extreme of sharing a man in order to avoid a fight."

"I don't know what you mean, but I'm not in the habit of sharing my husband. Though thanks to you, I just lost my best friend."

"What I see is that you're not as worried about losing me as you are about losing her."

"What I see is that you're competing with Sara."

"Over what? Over which one of us is more important to you?"

"That's what it looks like."

"You're out of your mind. But if it makes you feel better to think this is some sort of competition, go right ahead."

"So what we have here is that you're in love with my best friend."

"You want to tell me what's wrong with you? Are you feeling a little masochistic now?"

"I need to know. I hope you don't expect me to understand, be patient, and on top of all that, to keep my mouth shut."

"The two of you together scare me, but not as much as when you throw in Cristina. Then I really feel like splitting."

"Well, it doesn't really seem that way, Marco. You haven't left the house. You gave Sara a job and fell in love with her knowing that she's very close to Cristina. It looks like you're attracted to all three of us. Why don't we just become your harem? I ask myself what you'd like to do with Maura . . . ?"

"You all really scare me."

"It should be the other way around. *You're* Dracula, not us. But tell me, why do we scare you?"

"Together you have a sort of energy I don't understand very well. And I don't know where it comes from. And even though you all seem to be fighting, there's nobody that can split the three of you up."

"You're using a concept I don't like."

"What concept?"

"The concept of division."

"Do you see how you react when faced with that possibility?"

"What possibility?"

"The possibility of ending your friendship."

Elsa looks at Marco, faces him: "I'm sorry but there's no chance of that, so you might as well get used to it."

Marco gets on his feet, throws the sweater against the bed, and tries to intimidate Elsa: "Are you going to tell me what you talked to Sara about or not?"

And Elsa's indignation: "Who are you to interrogate me about my conversations with my friend Sara? What's it to you anyway? Why do you have to get between us? It's becoming more and more clear to me: you're trying to use the most vulgar of strategies, which consists of dividing us to gain an advantage. Can I tell you something? At this point I have to ask myself . . . I think it's important for all of us to know, I don't know, I ask myself what it is I like about you. What it is that's still keeping me in this relationship. I ask myself why I love you."

Marco's nervousness moves him from one side to the other like an electric train: "You can find out, if you've got a couple of minutes after trying to take Lucas away from me twenty-four hours a day while I'm trying to keep the family together. You can find out, if you've got a couple of minutes, after seeing all those women, your little prison buddies, to build that relationship you all have, which nobody can come between, most of all us men."

"I'd like to know what men you're talking about. The only man in this story is you. Cristina's husband is missing, maybe it's too much to ask you to remember that small detail . . . And Sara's husband is in jail, which must really make you happy. You're the only one who's free, with the possibility and the inclination to play these games."

"Thanks, Elsa, for reminding me that I never had any problems. But look, don't even bother trying to dump your feelings of guilt for being alive onto me. You won't succeed. Besides, while we're on the subject of good and bad memories I'd like you to remember who took care of *your* son when you were in jail, who brought the cotton for *your* periods, cigarettes, and news about Lucas. Who visited *your* mother . . . Please, think about it. But sure, now that you're out of jail, now that you have your freedom, and all its possible rewards, your first thought is Lucas. You're blind. You're so caught up in *your* reality that you're incapable of understanding that to 'get Lucas back' means taking him away from where he is emotionally and sticking him in a new place. Elsa, don't you see? You were away years and not days. And while you were in jail, I did everything for you and him that was possible while feeling the vulnerability of this 'freedom,' after working just to get by, to feed Lucas and help your mother, and after spending so much time answering all the questions that Lucas spent years asking me about what was going on. Now I'm alone. I don't know how this comes off sounding to you, but I really don't care. It's the truth. I'm alone. You come back after years of absence, and all you see is Lucas. What about everything else? What about everybody else?"

Elsa observes Marco. Marco observes Elsa. To a rhythm. They study each other to a rhythm they know very well.

There's a beat that is familiar to them, one that had been absent for years. Elsa feels it coming back. Now. And she sees Marco walk toward the bed, walk as if relieved, lie down beside her, and place his head on her feet, which are still bare and white. And Elsa concentrates on that image, on that roundness of the backside of Marco's head, now attached to the insteps of her feet, white, bare. And now she feels, This is the time, this is the right time to set conditions:

"What I'm going to tell you has nothing to do with generosity. But I don't know, if you stopped loving me, if this relationship is so deteriorated, if everything that happened during all these years affected you to the point where you can't go on . . . That's fine, Marco. This is so hard on everyone. And for you too. Don't think I don't know that. So listen, I'm just going to ask you to be honest, and let's avoid any unnecessary pain. That way, it'll be easier for me and for Lucas. Think about him. That's all I ask of you. And leave. Your presence here doesn't make sense anymore."

"I can't understand how you can be so flip, just like getting rid of old, dirty clothes . . . "

"And tell me . . . How did your affair with Sara get started? Was it very hard? Or not so hard?"

"I have no way of knowing what you've been talking about with your friend, but it seems what you call my 'my affair with Sara' has assumed monstrous proportions in your head. And monsters don't exist."

"Oh, sure. So monsters don't exist. Would you mind telling me, please, what you're trying to convince me of now? What you say is true, Marco. Nothing is forever, and there are events that define the directions life takes. Please, don't think this doesn't hurt me. It does. But I don't have the energy to change the natural inclinations of anyone. Let's not drag this out. We'll talk to Lucas and then you can leave."

"Prison changed you, Elsa. You don't love me anymore. I'm sure that if I'd gone through the same experiences as you, you'd consider me a hero and not a fool. Or at least you'd respect me. Your friends and your son hold a privileged place in your life. Of course this doesn't make me happy, but I don't have the energy to alter the natural course of anyone's feelings either. I'm too tired. And alone."

"Alone? What about Sara?"

"I'm alone. I feel alone."

Elsa's irony: "And I left you. And I don't love you anymore. Poor little Marco. And how did you arrive at the brilliant conclusion that I no longer love you?"

"You don't care about anything. Since you were released your only issue, your only point of reference, your only activity, the only reason you have for crying or laughing is Lucas. I don't represent anything for you. Absolutely nothing."

"He's my son and I was absent for four years."

"I wasn't."

"I haven't forgotten that."

"But you don't take it into account."

"Are you in love with Sara?"

"I will be if you go on acting this way."

"Oh, I get it. So now you're using Sara to make me be what you want me to be. Right? I'm just wondering if when all this started between you and Sara, you already knew the reasons why you were getting close to her. I'd like to know if she knew it. Or if she knows it now."

There's no answer that Marco can give in words. Marco knows few things at this moment. He knows that he's lying on his bed, and that his bed is their bed. He knows that Elsa is occupying her side of the bed, sitting and still hugging her knees. He knows that she's barefoot, and that he's been resting his head on those toes and the insteps of her feet for some time now. He has the feeling that when he rested his head on Elsa's feet, they were cold. But now it seems they're warm. And Marco knows almost nothing now, but something commands his movements and makes him raise his hands and squeeze Elsa's feet, makes him rub his cheek against them.

Other feet rest.

(ELSA AND MARCO'S VERSION,
IN THEIR CAR PARKED NEAR THE
COMMAND POST AT THE II ARMY CORPS)*

What are we doing here, together, looking out for Sara, so afraid of what might be happening behind those walls, desperate to see her come out, walk, move like any human being on the street, fretting over the possibility that she might not appear, that she might never emerge from that fortress of horror? What are we doing thinking about her, making an effort to imagine

---

* One of the five divisions of the Argentine Army, each responsible for a specific region of the country. The II Army Corps had its headquarters in Rosario.

the commander of the II Army Corps bristling as he tells her that she has to leave the country because if she stays they'll kill her, because she, just like Cristina and the rest of them, is too much of a threat to national security? What are we doing guessing some of the thousand answers she's capable of giving to those ultimatums, those sentences? What are the two of us doing, inside our car, our arms around each other? What are we doing? Maybe we're already in a position to give ourselves a unique and enviable response: we watch over Sara.

(SARA AND ELSA'S VERSION, IN THE TRAIN
THAT WILL TAKE SARA FAR AWAY)

"What a mess . . . "

"Sara, listen, that was just a very tiny part of all this horror. And, if you think about it, my being away all those years. You being so beautiful, honest, intelligent and sophisticated, crazy and ballsy . . . Me getting out of prison and completely dedicated to getting Lucas back again. How could Marco not fall in love with you? And you, with Hugo in jail, love-starved, like anyone else, you get your freedom and are alone, how could you not be tempted by someone like Marco? Warm, protective, a good person. He's very weak now, after all these years. I have to take care of him; I have to be very careful. And you know what? You were right: you and I know a lot about life . . . We know so much. You take it easy now. Protect yourself. We don't want any more martyrs. Go. Los Angeles. Santa Barbara. There are friends over there. International organizations. Give them the lists of the disappeared. You're right. We know so much."

"You have no idea how much I refused to acknowledge

reality, how much Marco and I tried not to see what was happening."

Elsa's open hands cup the sides of Sara's face. They turn Sara toward her, forcing her to look at her.

"Sara, all of us have been very strong, but we've suffered a lot. We're still suffering. And I love you."

The jackets tremble. They shake. They walk.
They face death.

Sara, What Does a Jacket Mean to You?

What is *that* question supposed to mean? Doesn't do a thing, at least not for me. It doesn't even make me want to look for an answer. I'm not hounding you with esoteric demands. And this question I'm going to put to you is one that, yes, would be healthy for you to give some kind of answer to: What's wrong with you anyway? And then come the pertinent variations: Why do you spend your time amusing yourself with the digressions you provoke me into making, why do you provoke these digressions, why don't you do something useful, why don't you just leave my head alone and go home and sleep? Why is it that when you're bored, the only thing that comes to mind is *I'm going to talk to Sara*. Better yet, I'm going to make Sara talk. Because you, you're so nice and quiet. I should have picked another line of work. Show business, for example. This bit about being a political exile and, to make things even worse, a writer, I don't know, it doesn't seem to be doing me any good. With the addition of friends like you—the kind of friend that, instead of pulling for the complete recovery of someone, instead plays a large part in their imbalance. Like you weren't an ex-prisoner and exile yourself. Like you didn't know what really screws people up and what helps them out. And then on top of everything, out of nowhere with that hair. Explain something to me, why *mahogany?*

Oh sure, you just had to roll your eyes. If you don't like to hear the truth, then I don't know what it is you keep looking for. And it's not just that hair. Because now you think you're a redhead, it means now you'll have to wear green eye makeup. Wouldn't want to be lacking in contrast, would we? I just might tell you, I don't buy it. But it seems life always travels in good company. It brings with it all kinds of resources against boredom. Including certain degrees of schizophrenia.

And the woman comes along, plops down in my only recliner, which by the way is black, my favorite color, with her mahogany hair, freshly permed, and her eyelids twinkling like emeralds, relaxes her legs and arms as if she carried around in her innermost self the spirit of María Teresa of Austria, and starts up the interrogation. How contemptible. I don't know how I put up with you. Oh well, like Vinchu said between mighty sighs during the '78 World Cup—you must have heard her as she roamed through the expanses of the Villa Devoto jail—"You have to pay. You have to pay. You have to pay. Every good deed is a luxury, and you have to pay. This soccer tournament is a punishment. You have to pay." And she twisted up, in disgust, every last muscle in her face. And she was right. Nothing is free. To love you as a friend brings with it daily unexpected consequences that put everyone at risk, including your own physical well being. I don't know if you've picked up on this urge of mine, which invades me at least three times a day, to strangle you slowly. Stop rolling your eyes or you'll make me go blind.

Look at the question. What is a jacket? And you, Chana, what do you think, huh? What does a jacket represent for you? Of course, you don't know. Though I will certainly give you some credit. You'd have a complete answer for me if I asked you for the best salon in the *Zona Rosa**, the address—including the zip code—what hours they're open, the names of all the employees as well as their personal problems. I have to admit; in that you definitely know your stuff. You're infallible. Infallible and ineffable.

You don't know what a jacket is. I hope you're not bringing up the subject because your intention is that at the end of the conversation I'll end up loaning you my leather jacket, for which I spent many, many hard hours working. Don't even think about it. Not even to go out dancing in. Every time I lend you something, it disappears. I understand your generosity, your unselfishness, your altruism, I understand your theory—concrete reality—that there's always someone with fewer means than you. But now listen, in this instance we're talking about *my* means.

Absolutely out of the question. I won't lend it to you.

Besides, this jacket has an importance for me that would be very difficult for you to imagine. It keeps me warm, you know? And you have to take care of what keeps you warm. But look, don't think all jackets can be described as favorably. Take for

---

*Refers to the "Pink Zone" in Mexico City, a tony area of the city known for its boutiques and restaurants.

example the denim one I had a few years ago. It was so unpleasant. Always so out of sync. I liked the color, though. But when it came time to use it for what it was really meant, it just couldn't hack it. The wind, like crushed ice, whipped through the sleeves, through the neck, and sliced right through my skin, totally unchecked. The jacket never really conformed to the shape of my figure. It was like body armor. It chose to rebel. Very nice looking, though nothing but image. And I gave it away. Because to rebel requires good reasons. Good reasons. Of course I'd like to know exactly what a good reason is, and who's the owner of such a measuring stick. Because the truth is that even the most unrecognizable reason would sound to me like an excellent opportunity, too good to waste by just dropping it into the hands of all those who aren't deserving of it. The ability to exceed limits is a privilege. Not everyone is capable of such deviation with an aplomb and elegance that magically turns excess into an incorruptible right. To resist takes effort, an investment of energies. And that physical and mental drain is not reserved for those who have learned to bleed with the kind of dignity that compromises you forever. That's why thinking about that denim jacket makes me sleepy. Because it humiliated itself trying to be something it wasn't. And people like that bore me. I know we're not talking about a human being. Though to tell you the truth, certain human beings are not easily distinguishable from a jacket. And certain jackets seem to have attitudes. The attitudes of certain human beings.

There are jackets that are a part of some people. And not just because they put them on, wear them. No. Nor because there are people who have the right kind of face that goes with a certain style of jacket, as is sometimes the case with certain names. Like what happened to me with that regular prisoner I was with for a few days just after they arrested me. Things like that tend to happen to me. Just before entering the ward, when I was still sort of spying on all of them from the corridor in the basement, trying to figure out where I was, I saw her face. I saw her face and thought: this woman must have a name with many *a*'s in it. Adriana. Her name must be Adriana. It couldn't be Viviana, it couldn't be Claudia. Adriana. She had the face of an Adriana. Stop rolling your eyes. Please. And it was true, her name was Adriana. Can you believe that? You don't believe anything. I know. Oh well. Strictly speaking though, the only important thing is that I know it. That I don't forget it. Because it has to do with me. With who I am. A tricky subject for you, I bet, who at thirty-two years of age has not yet discovered if you're a blonde, a brunette, or who knows if you didn't really come into the world sporting that hair you showed up with today, so proud, that we better not find out which hole in the wall ("salon" in your fearless streetcorner slang) in Mexico City you got your hair done. Am I right? She, Adriana, those eyes, that full mouth she had, the way she treated the rest of the prisoners, everything came attached to her name like she'd been born with it. There are people like that. There are people who are way too consistent.

People who wear clothes that seem like an extension of their umbilical cord. People you couldn't possibly imagine dressed in red, or white. People you wouldn't connect to a pair of sandals. To hair pulled back in a bun. To a jacket. Jackets. Jackets are incredible. There are people who are nobody, or nothing, without a jacket. Or without a cassock. Or without a hat. Or without their nails painted.

All that baggage. It's as if being naked, or being difficult to recognize, or not being at all, is just unacceptable. One cassock is not that different from another. But jackets are. They can be extremely different, even if they look the same. At least for me. I mean, Hugo went around so happy with his jacket during the winter and fall. And even though it wasn't one of those long ones, the kind that covers your ass, it was soft and thick and smooth, and when you put it on it felt like you were being smothered in an electric blanket. There wasn't one place where even a single drop of air could get through. It was black. That was very important. For Hugo it was fundamental. And when he was wearing it he was always checking out the cuffs. He looked at them, fascinated by the colored stripes in the weave. He ran his fingers over them. What I'm getting at is that he had developed a very symbiotic relationship with his jacket. When we needed it, we had it. And in the best way.

But when that asshole put it on, when that slimy sludge oozing from the cracks of the world decided to make contact with Hugo's jacket, with its warmth, with its black color and the multicolored cuffs, the story changed like you could have changed the date of a party. Just like that. And don't think it didn't hurt to restructure my feelings. You had to be able to readapt. You had to be capable of telling yourself, *That jacket isn't the same as before.* Like having to tear out a cancerous growth with your own nails.

To see him walking, or driving around in that car he or his little work buddies had stolen, the one in which he'd probably murdered I don't know how many *compañeros,* seeing him seated across from me in any café, at any moment, popping up just like that, appearing with that face of someone who owns half the universe and then some, of someone who has all that power and all the privilege to exercise it. Just like that, out of nowhere, and with Hugo's jacket. Not carrying it around, but wearing it. Wearing it. And Hugo in prison without any way of knowing, without the slightest idea that this guy had been wearing his jacket for the last four winters. Taking it over. Filling, invading that space which didn't belong to him. Almost like peeling off Hugo's skin and covering himself with it. I said covered. I didn't say *protected*. You can understand if I'm not up to bearing so much semantic weight right now.

Or no. Maybe not. Maybe he only started wearing it as a way of welcoming my freedom, you know, as if to say, Careful, I'm still here, and it just so happens I haven't forgotten about any of you. Either one of the two possibilities. Take your pick. It's the same story.

Chana, I'm kind of confused. Don't be offended; it's not that I don't realize full well that you're sitting here in front of me. That I do know. But it's not that simple. It's just that sometimes I don't know if I'm talking to you or your hair. It really fascinates me. I told you not to get offended. After all, I feel like I can't even confess my feelings to my own best friend. Whenever you finish with that audible fluttering of your eyelids, I'll continue.

Oh yes. So that's what I was telling you. That it's the same story. But you don't really know, nor do I want you to know what that year in Rosario was like. The ones who were set free in Buenos Aires didn't have it so bad, because they could pass unnoticed through the crowds, traffic jams, and the general accumulation of circumstances. It's easier to get lost, as you know, and also to escape the paranoia. Although nothing prevents our brilliant enemies from accomplishing their goals—that is, if you could say they had any. Goals for which we collected some hundreds of thousands of pieces of evidence. But in Rosario, to survive after prison in a city with one million people, when just by walking the streets at the same time you fatally encounter the same faces, the same feet, and consequently the same pistols (and if you don't see them, it's because they lurk, always on the muscle, under a sweater or, of course, a jacket)—now, that was difficult. And I know it was just as bad or worse in Córdoba. San Juan, Tucumán, the south, a successive collection of hells.

Look, Chana: everything—the everyday, the intimate, the barely perceptible variations we used to orchestrate in order not to succumb to boredom—was all so difficult to carry out. At one point for Cristina and me, and in a different way for Elsa too, finding certain pretexts to give us access to life became an obsession. Each circumstance, each event, dropped us more or less into the same forms of defense. Inevitably. We'd meet in the afternoon, after work. We'd get something to drink at a downtown café. Cristina and I. Elsa only sometimes: she was putting in a little quality bonding time with her son, highly effective, by the way. But the two of us, with Hugo in jail and Cristina searching for her disappeared husband, alone—though always with the unconditional affection and dedication of friends— saw each other continuously. We needed each other. We had each other.

Just about everything was working against us. The afternoon, the afternoon air. The shape that the light between the buildings took on. The walls outside. Inside. Everything smelled as though it didn't belong to us. The conversations we heard among the people walking through the streets, at the tables around us at any given café; their worries: what kind of car or motorcycle, what brand name was hot (not what model or brand they'd like to buy, because the severity of the economic bloodletting didn't allow for anyone with an iota of good sense to delude themselves so). Everything was unfamiliar: the nature of the activities in which even the youngest ones invested their time, the languid rhythm of the clouds moving across the sky. Everything. The blind silence of the ones who had given in to fear, and the memory loss of the ones brainwashed by the continuous practice of the most basic defense mechanisms. Everything alien. Everything hostile. We, who had been swallowed up by the tentacles of a monster we'd sensed close by, our activities, our youth suppressed from a hopped-up society, would reappear years later. We reappeared valiantly. But we fell, stunned and hounded by nausea, in the middle of the resounding deafness of a people deadened by fists. And it gave us a good dose of sadness and anger, though I'm not sure how effective a dose it was. Because in the middle of this unremitting pain, other vile matters weighed upon us: the check-ins at the command post of the II Army Corps, and the guy with Hugo's jacket following us around. Hugo, who couldn't get his freedom. Cristina's husband, who never appeared, obviously.

You had to be there, believe me. The *milicos,* who gave us the original "option" of leaving the country to go directly abroad, put an end to your exotic though dangerously effective political movement throughout the various hangouts in Córdoba. (Córdoba: the third, now pay attention, the third city of the country, and not the second. The second is and always was Rosario, even if it kills you to acknowledge that fact.) And for the paths we chose for our lives to take, you drew a rather dry stretch of road, sweetie.

The thing is that all through 1979, and I imagine the following years as well, the *milicos* weren't exactly willing to lose sight of Cristina and me. They had denied us the possibility of leaving the country so they could keep a hold on us. That's how I was able to get my freedom under surveillance for six months, and thanks to that freedom came the persecution during the whole period afterwards. The guy who had raided my house along with his crack group of experts, the guy who beat my body for hours, the one who made me listen to the version of Hugo already dead, the one who destroyed the furniture, who stole my panties and bras, my books, my typewriter, Hugo's clothes, and above all his jacket, the guy who deposited me sweetly and graciously in the basement of the police station, that same one, he and he alone, was again an active agent in the organization of my daily life. There were few places I went, alone or with Cristina, where he didn't pop up, as if right out of the ground, with those outlandish dark sunglasses, which of course no longer served the function of helping him avoid being recognized by me but accomplished, rather, the exact opposite intention. Cristina said that there must be a reason he chose to go around disguised as a fly. And with that dark hair. And Hugo's black jacket. Wearing it. Always wearing it. Even as the Rosario heat was wearing us all down.

Cristina. Cristina cleared up the vision of the world for me. She broke open the confines to which winds from all directions had subjected us, winds that stunned us, that dazed us, she broke them open, she broke them open, I swear, and cleared the way.

And we continued our movement. We pressed forward. With Cristina pursuing the nonexistent traces of her husband, by then perhaps also nonexistent. And me with my own companion in jail; and with so much life coursing through me, pleading with me to accept its presence.

Cristina, with all her dancer attributes, with that deep, artistic, and volatile mind that let her propel her body toward the uppermost reaches of the sky, was the one who hovered over me, who let me know that my feet had gotten too far off the ground, who explained to me that I had to come back, or, without theorizing too much, simply dragged me toward reason. Cristina was my measuring stick in reality.

The guy with Hugo's jacket had come to stipulate, to circumscribe our lives within some unimaginable point. It was impossible to ignore him. If at any time we decided to forget him, go to a movie theater, lose ourselves in a film, in its colors, in its movement, he'd be there when we left the theater, blending in with everyone around us, that face behind those insectoid sunglasses, the jeans, and Hugo's jacket, leaving us paralyzed. In any café. On any street.

And the check-ins at the command post. If you chose not to go, you of course went right back to jail, or were found dead on any sidewalk, in any ditch. You had to be punctual. No other choice. Each threat, each sign from the *milicos* that they knew even the most insignificant detail about what was going on in our lives multiplied the terror and the hatred. They wanted me to leave the country, yet they wouldn't give me a passport. They wanted Cristina to stop asking for the whereabouts of her husband. The *milico* told me with proverbial clarity: "She better not search anymore, because if she finds something, whatever it is will have a rotten smell." Enough said. They suspected Elsa of involvement in clandestine political activities. It seemed very strange to that bastard that she hadn't looked for work yet, that she spent her time only trying to rebuild her relationship with her son. And did he hound her about that, all the while Elsa was suffering and having anxieties that were more than justified, which someday I'll share with you, as soon as you get rid of that mahogany color from that empty head of yours. And I still don't quite get how it manages to stay connected to the rest of your body.

That *milico* also established the connection—a very clear one too—between himself and the orders he would give, and the guy in the jacket. Everything was indisputable, to such an extreme that I had to make some kind of decision. But don't think it was so easy. To leave the country, to leave Hugo in jail, the *compañeras* awaiting their freedom, to leave Cristina by herself (who never would have agreed to give up searching for her *compañero*), and all our other friends, who had been such a great help.

But look, we didn't have to sit around thinking about it too much. Things got moving. The *milico* told me to try again to obtain a passport. That maybe they would give me one. Of course it only hinged on an order—or counterorder—that he'd give over the phone from his desk. And that's how it was. After months and months of my insisting, they gave it to me.

At any rate, in my mind and Cristina's it wasn't easy to accommodate resignation just like that: we still planned on renting an apartment together. And on the day I went over to let Cristina show it to me—she was working for a real estate agency—and just as we were about to look at the bedrooms, just the two of us in there, someone began pounding on the door, trying to force it open. Cristina wasn't expecting anyone. Frightened, she turned the key to unlock the door, but the person waiting on the other side pushed against the door first, crashed in, and slammed the door shut. And there he was, with Hugo's jacket. Wearing it.

He closed in on us quickly. With one hand he grabbed Cristina by the hair, and with the other he clutched the pistol he was carrying under the jacket. He told Cristina to stop looking for her husband, because if she wasn't careful she'd wind up just like him. And after foaming just enough from the mouth, he ordered us down on the floor. Once we were both arranged to the fancy of his delicate tastes, one next to the other, he started to leave. When he reached the door he peeled off the jacket. And showing off his great histrionic talents, kind of like the gestures of a mime on acid, he threw it against my face. Then he said to me: "Keep it as a souvenir."

As a final number, it would have been so much more effective for the guy if the wall across from us—near where we lay sprawled on the floor—had been covered with a large mirror. We would have seen ourselves, and surely it would have been so hard for us to believe what we were seeing. Everything's kind of sketchy, but we must have looked pale, suddenly emaciated. And totally paralyzed. No: maybe not totally. Because Cristina, as usual, even in the middle of the storm, picked up what was going on. While both of us were still lying there without having the sense to stand up, she looked me straight in the eye and said: "Sara, I'm going to miss you."

And me, what could I do, tell me, with that jacket? I stared at it dumbfounded. I looked it over with my eyes, without moving to touch it with my fingers. I moved my legs, letting the jacket slide off onto the floor. The cuffs weren't faded. It looked like the same jacket from four or five years ago. Maybe the leather wasn't as shiny. I don't know. I'm not sure. An aversion filled my eyes. It went up and down and through my digestive system. It was all an overwhelming nausea.

We left there with a mixture of fear, sadness, and hate; all three combined to form a highly potent fuel that propelled us into action.

A few days later, when my suitcases were just about packed and ready to go, I went to visit Hugo in prison. To say good-bye. And I took him the jacket. After all, it was his and nothing more than his. I showed it to him through the glass of the visiting booth, and he didn't understand. He didn't know a thing. Not even the fact that years earlier the cops had taken it. I told him I'd leave it so he could get it from the guard. I also asked him to please never, ever wear it. Only to keep it. That whenever he got out and whenever we met somewhere in the world I'd tell him everything that had happened with it. He just looked at me. He looked at me confused. I made some gestures—I'm sure they looked silly and didn't explain a thing—and he knew I couldn't speak into the microphone, because whatever they picked up would be translated into a royal beating when he returned to his cell, into a month of solitary confinement, or into just who knows what sophisticated innovation. And everything was left just like that. Half finished. Hanging. And suddenly I, too close to his pain and to my tears, turned around and left quickly, unable to look behind me one last time, which is what all of us prisoners wanted so much from our visitors. Do you remember? That last good-bye. That final look.

Something strange is happening. I don't get it. May I ask why you're not rolling your eyes as you should be doing to the heavy stuff I'm telling you? There, just like that. Thanks.

When he finally arrived in Los Angeles a year later we were, predictably, different. Along with all the other anguish, he hadn't included the jacket among his things, not even in the most remote corner of any of his suitcases. He'd left it behind. Can you believe it? You'll tell me he didn't know the story behind it. Sure he didn't. But he must have understood something about the shape, the power of the enigma I'd tried to convey to him on that last prison visit. I was his companion. And he hadn't caught my intensity. When I asked him what he had done with the jacket he answered that he couldn't remember if he had left it at his mother's house, or my mother's house, or his brother's house. I told him the long story, my emotions spilling out. You know how I am. His response was: "And what problem do you have with that now? Let it go. A jacket's a jacket, nothing more, nothing less." And he repeated: "Let it go." Then I realized I was in front of the same old Hugo who, six years before, confronted by my intuition, my certainty that we were going to be arrested—the one always skipping out the door, always on the move—told me I should stop my crazy delusions and get out of bed as he handed me one last maté.

We lived together for a year and a half. We spent that time in different ways, exploring the relationship; the possibility of the relationship. But no, Chana. I just couldn't.

The world had completed its turning too many times during those years. And no movement is in vain. Not a single one.

When the divorce had gone through he called me, completely broken up, so sad. He asked me what I'd felt when I signed the papers, realizing everything between us was finished. I answered him with another question. A tricky one. Out of line. I said: "And you, what did you feel when I told you all about the travails of your leather jacket, the one you, we, had loved so much?" He didn't have an answer.

So here I am, Chanita. In your beloved Mexico. The Mexico of your exile. For a year, maybe two. I don't know. Afterwards I want to go back to Los Angeles. To Santa Barbara. The celebrated Mexico City fills me with curiosity, anxiety. But I write a lot. I write and write. That is, when you don't come to visit me. With that hair. Go on, roll your eyes a bit, because when you leave them still for too long I get dizzy. Now I've got this identity crisis; I stop knowing who I'm with, who I am. I lose my way. Come on. Just a little.

And about that loan, forget it. There is no jacket. I have no plans to run the risk of losing another one. Besides, if it got lost, it wouldn't be on account of my own misadventures, but yours. Do me a favor, stop rolling your eyes. I said no.

The letters fly.

Letter to Aubervilliers

For Juliana, who is Estela

Santa Barbara, 20 January 1984

What kind of effect will these sorts of aftershocks, or whatever you want to call them, have on you down the road? (It's never too late, dear!), since they're like needles located in strategic points throughout the brain. What I mean is that catharses never come alone: the Paraná River flows from the Matto Grosso, dragging along with it a variety of specimens. The water lilies, Juliana, and the piranhas. The water lilies I'm fairly sure about. But I wonder why the piranhas never reach Rosario.

We are moving along fluidly through the first days of 1984. And also quickly. Others are able to detach themselves from accumulation, and from the years. I thought about sorting through those events always willing to linger behind. This isn't by accident. Don't you go believing in accidents. I'm trying to stick myself at the vanishing point of every possible vision in order to begin a story whose axis would be our transfer from the basement in Rosario to Villa Devoto.

Even if I turn myself inside out like a glove trying to get over all of this.

So there you have it. Once I asked you to write me, answering my questions about your torture. We both could tell even by the inflections in your voice in those situations. But I felt compelled, by my request and by your answers, and proceeded with the novel I was writing. Now, the same ploy.

Last night I couldn't sleep well: that bit about the kid being born with some sort of defect. And this morning on the way to work, when the two of us had already left the house, I realized I was still back inside, looking for the front door.

Santa Barbara is wild and revels in it. The town spreads her legs and quivers from the sun and excess. No one ever dies here. On the other hand the Paraná River, you know, kinks our nerves. The snakes and everything else it dumps on us when it has run its due course. Does this ring a bell? *The Paraná originates in Brazil where the Paranaíba and the Grande Rivers meet.* That I still dredge up this memory must be the result of some intravenous injection given to me by the old crone from geography class. There's no other way to explain it.

From the basement to Villa Devoto. Impossible to recall everything. Oh sure, certain moments of anguish: Blanca always had the shadow of a mustache that was more pronounced than the recommendable shade. That particular day it really blackened her out, cutting her face in half. She was handcuffed to Tania. Tania so tall and the other one so short, with her mustache and all her personal belongings in a blue sack made from jeans by a pair of those almost magical hands we were all beginning to develop. Tell me a little about Paris. OK? Isn't that where you live? Or are you locked up in the bathroom of your apartment? Or in the kitchen? I hope you're in the bedroom.

Your street must be like one of those in Posadas. Cobblestones, plants sprouting up between the stones, and, on the occasional leaf, a foraging ant at full gallop. That's what I picture a street to be like in Posadas; aside from being splashed by the swell of the Paraná when it goes crazy. Birds' cries, broken beer bottles, incestuous and promiscuous rains must also splatter the other streets of Paris. And the Paraná, too, just a wee bit, I'm sure. Help me confirm this. Thanks.

Who were you cuffed to? I don't recall seeing anyone next to you at the time. But what I'll never forget, when we got to Devoto, was when Mercedes entered the ward we'd been assigned and promptly vomited her heart out. With that gesture she sent everything resembling that transfer of political prisoners and its possible implications down the bathroom plumbing. Sublime.

Ward 31! I'm serious. Sublime.

I wonder where Flora is; the one who would wash her own clothes when it was anyone's turn but hers and then would hang them from the only clothesline in the bathroom without thinking twice about it. I wonder what's become of that pinchy face of hers. She's probably selecting the appropriate laundry detergent or bars of soap somewhere in Senegal. It is possible that after so many years of exile she might have acquired a washing machine. Though it depends: I don't know what degree of training she may have received.

Your mother wrote me for my birthday. She comes across like a flower at nine in the morning of a Buenos Aires summer. I don't mean to be redundant, but I envy you. A mother like Adelina!

One lives apologizing. Fear of being repetitive. Ask the *milicos* if they cared about repeating methods, plagiarizing them, wearing them out. Okay then; don't even bother. Don't ask them a thing.

I feel like I'm focusing all my efforts on sticking my finger in some hole.

Our flag, the one we left hanging up in the bathroom of the basement just before they took us away. I don't know, I never quite completed the mental picture of the female guards' hands frozen in some form of utter surprise, suspended between the flag and their fat bellies, their tits, trying to decide whether or not to rip it down. To touch it, to embrace the devil. Not pale blue, white, and pale blue, dear: only pale blue and white. Can you imagine the guards? So pure, they were.

To embrace the devil. Fingertips getting closer. He must be hot all over, no matter where you touch him. Febrile eyes, and that pointed beard that fills you with a desire, I mean a real desire to lean up against him, don't you think? No doubt about it: if Lucifer ever shows his face, I'll give it a try. What a great little siesta! And forget about any *vade retros*. There must be a lot to learn from this.

Get between the sheets. The blankets weigh heavy on my right side. Yes. I'll take a shower and continue this from bed.

I was thinking—water is a sacrament—that making a resolution, choosing an option, is like voluntarily losing a finger on one hand and suddenly out of nowhere acquiring three on the other. Don't fret too much. You know: a warm-up. Remember the story to come. I'm opening the first hole. Though I could also just be taking a big leap. This is nothing new, I know. These leaps of mine give you pains in the liver, but you can see them coming. It's so great to be able to decide, to choose. Isn't it like singing "Yesterday," slowly modulating each word with your own lips, shaping them one at a time, using every muscle, your teeth, your tongue, your whole mouth, lying in a hammock from which the only vision might be a large, clear platter topped with violet cherries and a white airplane taking off?

Before the female guard cuffed me, to Sonia I think, and forced us down with a brutal shove onto the bare floor of the transport plane, she delivered, just like another punch, a "Don't look up!" I barely raised my head. Most of our *compañeras* were already lined up, sitting Buddha-style, chained to the metal floor, heads lowered and their free arm slung across the backs of their heads. I swear I took an eternal photo of this scene, for posterity's sake.

A formation, a squad in military position frozen in mid-movement, just at the moment of drawing in their heads, their arms, their legs in an intimate dance step, forming a full circle, only then to open up and extend themselves outward, forever. Don't tell me that reality on the airplane didn't look like any kind of dance. I already know that. It's really more like a historical dizziness, a universal nausea, which for all intents and purposes let us sense what direction this great digestive apparatus in which we live had decided to take.

The shackles and the handcuffs were the chicken and the egg; they were an absolute, a fiction. A feast of possibilities was offered up before all our eyes, all our lips repressing the urge to utter even a sound.

Some combat boots also unleashed their own form of expression, against our shoulders, our heads, among the faces that tried to readjust their perspective, capturing an angle of the whole and the resounding hardness of the heels. I was already in the military plane, bound from head to toe. Bonavena, our heavyweight champ, castrated. Imagine that.

It's been a long day. I've been trying to confront my work with a bit of our philosophical What can you do? But there's no room left for fantasies in these latitudes.

Suddenly, and only because of its buzzing, my attention was drawn to a pedantic fly, the likes of which have never been seen, a fly that spent fifteen minutes of its life—and mine— butting its head against the window. And don't come to me with that logic of yours; it really was pedantic. And I didn't set it on its way sooner because I stood there following it, watching it either in the process of breaking down, giving in, or following its unswerving dedication to the cause. You should have seen it turn around and then pick up speed again, heading straight for the light, until it finally cracked the windowpane from one side to the other. *This place reserves the right to refuse service to anyone. I won't bat an eye if you question the verisimilitude of all this.* Does this sound familiar?

The fly didn't leave on its own accord; it seems it got all dizzy and wasn't able to complete its mission. It landed on the window sill, shaken up, looking victimized; so I opened the window.

Tell me, Juliana: do you remember a white cotton dress, with black flowers, which looked so good on the both of us and which my old lady sewed for me after we were freed? Last night, while walking along State Street, I saw an almost identical one in a store window. It had just one effect on me: a desire to lash the air with a couple of my wicked shrieks.

And sometimes it gets so dirty around Rosario, the river, I mean—or so clean: the next task will be to establish specific limits—it's tempting to dive in, swim around underwater, because we all know what can get tangled up down there with the plants and the mud. What do you imagine is down there? Some irreplaceable treasures: I bet there's a Jimi Hendrix single, the *Anti-Dühring,* and a good thesaurus. A *good one,* because the better it is, the more useless it is. And the quicker you get rid of it.

We had to be ready in twenty minutes with a change of clothing. Where would we find the composure to forestall that eternity. In half the time we were already waiting, all of us linked together by a very real electrical current that kept our throats and stomachs charged. But do you know what's really so anguishing? The possibility that at that moment none of us understood the essence of the problem. But no, that's not exactly right either; because, if we couldn't grasp the pith of the matter, then tell me what it was that made us bid farewell as if we were going to die. We bore into each other with white stares, pieces of chalk firm against our foreheads, we studied our pale faces, our wrinkles, our recently acquired gray hairs; we fixed each other's hair, picked off loose threads and lint.

Some recollections have been amputated. But it takes very little effort to get my neurons going again; just reestablish the images and the sensations come back in one piece.

I got a letter from Virginia. The whole thing's about a motorcycle that her new companion bought; incredible as it may be, the letter's actually not boring. Maybe she'll find a way to ridicule that guy, Gustavo. You can tell there is something about him in a helmet that's incompatible with certain anxieties of hers. There was no way to get her off the subject. It says something that the motorcycle, the helmet, and the husband all charm her and repulse her at the same time; I don't know.

I've been making a serious effort to remember certain episodes. But no such luck. It's like a sheet hung between my eyes and my brain. The reason for the memory loss is all right there: in the colors, the shapes, the greater or lesser clarity, the rhythms. The lethal potential of events.

For example, the plane landing. I know we landed in Aeroparque because someone told me later on; I don't know

when. But I can't, I can't get that part of the movie. I go from
midflight to the prison trucks that transported us to Villa Devoto. The landing got cut out. What followed, right up until
the point when I began to move through the unmistakable
Buenos Aires steam, was also erased. I can still feel the as-
phyxiation, the rills of sweat skipping down my back, I feel the
dehydration as if right now they were trying to force me to
swallow a watermelon whole. With that intensity. I see gray
and green; the green and gray have stuck with me.

But there are great, unbridgeable gaps.

Hey you, it's getting late. I'm going to see if I can get some
sleep. My eyes are stinging: I broke one of the sidepieces on my
glasses. The cause: while in Mexico, I gave David the only good
case I had. Annie gave me an even better one, but the time in
between proved fatal. And with this I close. Write at once.
Time passes by fluidly. Also rapidly. (Did I already say that?)

The human being that is taking over the space inside of me
literally bends over backwards to be friendly. Patience: the
fight against cancer, history breaking away from the line of de-
sires, the military parades, the shadow cast against your house
by the building in front of it, these things moderate the spirit.

Ciao. Kisses to the known and loved ones we have in common. My love to you, as always.

Sara

P.S. That photo you sent me of your daughter holding a
chicken in her arms is so stupid that I can't for the life of me
figure out why you included it with the others, all of them
so beautiful. Kisses.

The rats walk and swim.

As in War: In War

"I wonder if there'll be a moon tonight."

"It got towed away."

"I mean, if we'll be able to see it." Brilliant! Here we go again. I knew it. Pulling guard duty with Gloria. Always the same. Arguments. Following my lady's orders. Acute neuro-hormonitis.

"I don't have an answer. I'm sorry. What was that noise?"

"It came from the back, by Silvia's bed."

"Let me check it out." Let me check it out, Liliana; let me check it out. My heels, the sticky floor, and yet I walk; let me check it out. Slabs of sleeping flesh, heads, arms, so vulnerable, easy, with just one blow, no cries; a shape on the floor: it's moving. No, nothing: paper. Let me see; the noise, what noise? By Silvia's bed, who sleeps soundlessly. All of them vulnerable but alive. Not dead: alive. Our children, from our legs; our children; cramped. Labored. The noise. A bird can't get in. Nobody went to the bathroom. Once there was that mouse rasping against the wood in the night, and I pretended not to understand, telling myself I was hearing creaking sounds, probably the wood expanding from the heat. Children of ours, what pains. It stinks. This ward is filled with smells.

"What was it?"

"Nothing. The kids are asleep. All of them."

"I wonder what time it is?"

"Why don't you ask me something I can answer? I mean, that way you won't get frustrated by your grand attempt at communication."

"It must have been more than two hours by now. Let's call the next guard." I'm tired. Two hours of putting up with you. I want to sleep.

"What's wrong? You're being a real pain in the ass."

"Must be that time of the month coming up. Forgive me, Your Majesty."

"When do they take your son back?"

"Monday. The three months will be up then."

"Who's going to take care of him?"

"The old woman: sixty-eight years old, all alone, sick. And to top it off she has to raise the kid."

"It'll make her happy."

"Jorge is my son. He's mine."

"If you're going to talk foolishness, you'd be better off just keeping your mouth shut: you're here, inside. That noise again. Did you hear it?"

"This time it came from the kitchen area, didn't it?"

"If the system would allow us to hang onto the kids longer they would get more used to us."

"Yeah. Then who would take him away from me?"

"Who'd take them away? Oh, that's a real tough one: the cops would, honey . . . Let me go to the back. I want to see what's moving around."

"Wake up the next pair."

"Stop pestering me." Same path, but along the next row of tiles. Put my foot down, try to pull it loose. Gum, impossible: only in freedom. Paste, impossible: only in freedom. Tar, impossible: only in freedom. Anything that sticks, that sticks to, only in freedom. Whatever enslaves, only in freedom. And here inside you're free, your head explodes only as many times as it's provoked, nothing quashes your skull. A bird is flying around. Or something: something is flying around. Something with a claw, a beak that snags a movement. A bird that skewers a rat to the floor with its beak.

"Well?"

"Nothing. Your son's sleeping with his mouth open."

"Again? I'll be right back."

"Don't make any noise." Your son's open mouth. Your open mouth. An open mouth: a cat's. Alive, not dead. Swallowing a rat. Gray. Ratty breath. Rat smell. Hair between the tongue and palate. Inside the mouth. Inside your open mouth. Which closes, Liliana.

"I'm dead tired."

"I'd prefer not to wake the girls up. It must be around two o'clock. I don't know about Claudia, but Olga was pretty beat. I can last until six. How about you?"

"I don't know. I'll try if you want. Jorge will be hungry around six. How about yours?"

"Around five-thirty."

"What was that?"

"Marta's breast-feeding Curi."

"OK, let's give it a try. That's odd: I haven't heard the female guard in the last hour. La Enana, I mean."

"She's teamed up with La Pelirroja today. By now both are probably drunk."

"Keep it down."

"What the hell's wrong with you today anyway?! Don't take it out on me that you're getting your period!"

"Shhh! I told you! Go stand up against the wall."

"What did you say? I didn't hear anything."

"Could you do me a favor and just shut up?"

"If you keep me informed."

"You want the guard to catch us?"

"No. I don't want that. And what guard? I told you, they're horsing around with the men."

"Why are we standing watch then?"

"To sample the evening air. I forgot the white wine. Everything else is just right."

"And to see to it they don't try to take the kids away from us in the middle of the night."

"You got it."

"Somebody's coming." Who is it? Saliva gets caught in my throat. What's going on? The steps are loud. Calm down now: Gloria's going to make fun of me.

"La Pelirroja. Oh shit! She's wearing high heels. Be careful: she's close." High heels. The red rat's wearing high heels. Her hind legs trying to support the weight of her body; tense, veiny legs. A red rat with tresses. Rats with red tresses. Rats in red dresses. Dressy tresses on their hairy asses. How can I think of that? That isn't me. That wasn't me. Or maybe it was me but that wasn't what I thought.

"What's she doing?" What's she doing? Why? What does she want? Calm down, you chickenshit. Gloria the First can smell your adrenaline.

"She's gone."

"Here she comes again."

"Did she get a look?"

"She peeked in."

"Is she drunk?"

"Couldn't tell."

"What's going on?"

"It's too quiet. Do you think she heard us?"

"Listen. Did you hear that? She fell. The redhead fell down on the floor."

"Is she alone?"

"What do you care? They'll come to help her up soon enough. Don't worry about it."

"Oh look, this you have to see! She's carrying a serving bowl."

"A what?"

"La Enana came to her rescue. Look, the midget's carrying a glass serving bowl: she's going to drop it, it's falling! Oh look, right on top of La Pelirroja. Fruit salad! What a mess!"

"They woke the kids up."

"Fuckers."

"Tell Marisa not to get them out of bed. Tell her just to try and calm them down in their beds. But make sure they calm them down."

"You don't ask for a whole lot, do you?"

"Hurry up!" Always talking back. You're so slow. Have to tell you everything twice. Always putting that slow madness of yours to use. Your limp madness. Looking for any chance to slack off. But look at the rats; there are still some fast things around here, crazy speeds, speedy crazies. In Mexico City, they say, eight per person. Counting those incapable of reason. One for each left eye. One for each right eye. One for each foot. One for each tongue. One for each hand. One for each frigid erogenous zone. Eight speedies per person. Eight crazies per head. Per capita. Some day we'll walk through Mexico, if we survive the Argentine rats.

"Are you getting that crazy look on your face again?"

"Go help Marisa deal with that racket."

"You think they're going to calm them down just like that?"

"Go on, Liliana! Otherwise, the guards will come in and give us a wringing out."

"And you're going to stay here all alone?" The heroine. Of course. How is she going to cover herself? Expose her hide, be brave, be very brave!

"Here where?"

"By the bars."

"I'm on watch. What do you want me to do?"

"Move closer to the rear."

"You just take it easy." Poor thing. Relax! But she doesn't scoff at my suggestion. She's going to give it a try, even if she has no idea what peace is, peace and quiet, or even how to achieve that state. Don't walk like that. Let your arm hang loose, relaxed. Don't move it around. Our mediums are land and air. Nobody needs to swim here. Except the rats. Do rats swim?

"Marisa, wait, don't get up. I'll help you."

"What was that noise?"

"They're screwing around with the male guards. Imagine that."

"How do we get the kids to calm down now? Goddamned bitches. Almost all the kids are awake. Do what you can with these two. I'll work this side."

"Silvia's getting up. Tell her to get back in bed." Gloria will be furious.

"It's OK, Silvia. They're asleep again."

"I'll give you a hand. What happened?"

"Nothing. Go to bed. If you want, you can take your little girl with you."

"Who's standing guard?"

"On their side?"

"No, ours."

"Gloria and me."

"Go back with Gloria then. We've got this all under control."

"OK. Gloria! Everything's under control."

"Yeah." Under control. What did they stick into their mouths? It doesn't matter. Something. But they're breathing. Their mothers. Nothing else. Mothers in the mouths of their children. Tongues. Tongues shaped like mothers. A mother-eating baby. Baby and *milico* fighting over a mother: the best kind of war, it can't be covered up. The most exciting kind. Mother sleeping and waking up. Alert. Baby in danger. Mother leaping onto a huge *milico,* ripping out his eyeballs with her sharp fingernails. *Milico* falling into an eternal sleep, one with fairies, one with golden flamingoes. Baby crying with his pride wounded, it wasn't my victory, you didn't let me do it all by myself. I have to thank you, and I don't want to: die, mother. Kick the bucket. A baby swallowing a mother in a striped uniform. Surrealistic. And then I go and lose my tongue, the baby squawks. Realistic. Stick. Stick a fork in you, Liliana, you're just about done.

"What's wrong?" Must be looking out the corner of my eye. Teeth must be clenched. What's the answer going to be?

"As soon as they made it to their feet they came back with a broom and a mop. La Pelirroja kept insulting La Enana, telling her that the Chief of Security would find out about this, that if they gave her the sack, she would never forget what they did."

"The chief?"

"No, girl! La Enana!"

"If they fire the redhead they'll get rid of the entire guard."

"Except the one that rats on them."

"And?"

"They went back to their little party."

"It seems that a guy from Corrientes, the one who inspects the bars to make sure no one's trying to escape, fancies La Pelirroja."

"That's interesting."

"It's the latest from the third floor. They heard something. Scoot over."

"Another way of wasting your time."

"Give me a little room. We have to do something to keep ourselves entertained."

"Try being productive, darling. It does wonders for me."

"You're such a pill. You want to stay on guard so you can keep your bad mood?"

"These kids are amazing. They're all asleep again."

"Let's see how they behave on the outside."

"Well, it's going to be hard. Difficult, of course. At first. Andrea already recognizes me. She's going to notice the change. Hey, don't push me! Sit closer to the edge. What are you looking at with that face?"

"Why are you getting so hysterical?"

"That's crazy."

"You are."

"Don't be ridiculous, Liliana. Why don't you go to bed? You didn't feel like staying on guard anyway."

"Strength. Yes, you're so strong. I'm going to try really hard to follow your example."

"You'll have to resign yourself to a life of sacrifice."

"It's a good thing you're only kidding. Gloria and Perón:* one heart and not so far apart. Shall we move along, Your Majesty?"

"I mean if you want to find a small place in that heart."

"God save me, protect me, release me, guard me, etc. . . . "

"From the dregs of society!"

"From the love of your brothers . . . "

"How sacrilegious. What are you laughing at?"

"That's all we needed. Go on, tell me why you're so militant tonight."

"Don't go calling me something I'm not."

"Loosen up. C'mon, tell me. When do they take Andrea away?"

"Don't ask me if you already know."

* Juan Domingo Perón (1895–1974), president of Argentina from 1946 to 1955. He was elected president again in 1973 after spending eighteen years in exile.

"Fine; but at least talk. Let me help you out."

"You? What are you going to help me with? Besides, you're in the same bind."

"That's why I can help you. I've got the same ball inside me."

"Shit. That's what it is? A ball, right? A lead ball."

"It's like I've got a gallon of lye in my intestines. Lye. A metal door painted red. My old man wanted it white. Caustic soda at work. And me, barely three years old, a stupid little white dress with the 'traveling ants'* on the front, a real fan of danger; not conjuring it up: worshiping it. Standing there, all serious, my eyes sinking into that bucket, convinced that sooner or later the unstable liquid would provoke a family disaster."

"Are you reminiscing? Is that how it was?"

"Yeah, that's the way it was. I'm reminiscing."

"And?"

"No injuries. The following day he painted the door white."

"And what about you?"

"An irreversible feeling for caustic soda."

"And now it fills your intestines."

"Isn't that unfair?"

"Don't beat yourself up over it. The one who needed help was me. I could eat one of those Santa Fe pastries whole. All by myself. Glaze my belly, arms, hair with caramel. My feet."

"Look at the color of the walls."

"The sun's coming up. What a summer morning!"

"We have to get breakfast started. I'll go."

"You have to really water down the maté otherwise it won't

La hormiguita viajera (The traveling ant) is the title of a popular children's story. The characters also appeared on children's clothing.

be enough. Hey, Liliana! Make sure it boils: there's no milk for the kids."

This broken knob, any moment now the gas will start leaking and of course nobody is going to come and help us out. This pot is going to take a while to come to a boil.

Liliana fiddles with the knob as if she could fix it. She'll just end up breaking it, the klutz.

The baby bottles. The cups. First the baby bottles.

What's she doing? She lines up the baby bottles like they were telephone poles. Or toy soldiers. That's it: toy soldiers.

I'm going to the bathroom until this is ready.

Where's she going? To the bathroom.

The water is already boiling.

She already filled the bottles.

Now let them cool off a bit. A few minutes. A few short ones.

What the hell's she waiting for? Now she's passing them out.

There we go. They're starving. Look at them gulp it down! Come on, kiddies, eat up, suck down that exotic delicacy courtesy of the prison; enjoy it, darlings. You need the nourishment.

Look at them go! What a show! And now? Liliana, who pulls her duty in such a marvelous, efficient, and original manner on this day, passes back through picking up the empty bottles.

Now thy progenitors. The delicious cooked maté made from beets for thy little mommies.

What's wrong with her? What's she looking at?

I can't. No. The noise we heard. I have to scream and I can't. Huge. It's huge. As big as a cat. It was cooked. Its mouth half open. The kids. Will they live? What should I do? I have to react like an adult. Adult. She'll bitch me out. She'll laugh at me. She'll ridicule me. The rat. Gloria. I'm going to start walking toward the center of the ward, I'm going to announce it aloud, but with a serious expression. No hysterics. Mature. Now. I begin to walk. Like a mature *compañera*. It fell into the pot of maté. It drowned. Boiled alive. Walk upright. Like a true *compañera*. Standing tall and no inflections in my voice. No sign of hesitation on my face. Now: women, there's a rat at the bottom of the pot of cooked maté. Just like that, standing tall, trying to tighten my throat so my breathing won't give me away. My knees are trembling. Just like that. Serious. And the kids drank serious rat broth in their baby bottles. Serious. All boiled and bloated, its skin stretched taut, snooty looking, serious forever. Like a true *compañera*. That's the way I have to make the announcement about the rat. My hands steady, not a tinge of melancholy.

Death marches to its own beat:
it walks.

From Sara's Diary

For Alicia País, who was murdered

17 May, midafternoon

A must: I need the animal that's burrowing in my stomach to poison itself and die right now. (But then I don't want it peering out from my belly button with cadaver eyes.) It works away quietly, as if scraping through ice.

Any changes in the panorama? Who could think of such a thing? The tiny window above, the projection of metal cast stately across the ceiling, the orange sun stuck to the wall, both fighting to hold onto, grab onto one of those certain forms of loftiness so manipulable, so coveted by survival. I look at the bunks next to me: Silvina is working everyone over, intent on convincing the rest of us that she can concentrate and write a letter. And so conventional she is, throwing out her left hip, sucking on her right index finger as she repeats: "And if not then, expound for me the counterargument; and it better be very well founded." Leticia scrutinizes the watered-down tea with a more vociferous and less elegant disgust than was suitable to the ward's stomach; she begins to pass it around. Gri-

selda reads *The Plague,* though I can't believe it; she flashes
back to the moment when her son was the age in the picture
she hides inside the flap of her book. Something along the lines
of a trip around the world, all of this. I ask myself what I'm
doing here, why I don't just pass right through these walls with
all the calm and cheer I can muster. I ask you that, Sara. Yes.
Good way to put it: calm, cheer.

Same day, at night

They're about to cut the lights. Nothing to say. Just one thing:
ugh. I don't feel like getting into this. The investigations, the
references to the mechanisms we rely on immobilize me. They
force me to face the whole picture. They drown me in details.
They dump the whole abyss on me all at once. But that's okay.
Just this: that routine, unbearable to live by in human days, in
here keeps you clear of death. Novelty is a danger. Always.
Disproportion: a huge, deep purple hematoma that covers hundreds, thousands of bodies.

Sleep will be better for me tonight than on other nights. But
it still feels like this: that it's shitty to have nothing to say.

18 May, three o'clock, three-thirty in the afternoon: break time

Our spastic Andrea has just come in, heaving her shoulders up
and down. She doesn't understand that the only flights reserved for her are metaphysical ones. And with the news of the
day: a *compañera* from the second floor was taken to the emergency area of the prison hospital: Patricia Del Campo. I don't
know her. What is noticeable though is the anguished disorder
whipping around Andrea's propellers, which every now and
then resemble human arms. Dora and Elizabeth move about in
various directions through this 5×8 sliver of space. Dora looks

pale. Dora scares me. For me, she sums up a sizable chunk of existence. Her projects. The problem isn't what she proposes as a militant, with that tried and true line about how there are so many ways to contribute, but rather how she chokes on the process. She's so clinical about finding the whys, so against requesting a little extra growth from her own nose that just might get her closer to the facts. Action, and which bathroom is Dora peeing in? That's a liberty not all of us take: a piss while spying out the bathroom window. With sterilized glass and immaculate curtains made of fine lace. And then the leftover lace. For when the *milicos* set aside for us a good lacing across the mouth. Besides, yesterday she managed to stop me dead in my tracks when she talked about wanting to start up a noodle factory whenever she got out. Was that head case being literal?

And pay attention to the little moving pictures on the far wall, animated today by the sun. Round ones, oval ones. Like leaves. (These last two sentences just struck a chord in me. The palms of my hands got all clammy and my ears started to burn. I wonder what caused it.)

Same day, late afternoon

We had to bail the water from the first toilet on our side in order to get the phone to work. More news: Patricia Del Campo, good friend of the professional pisser. Hepatitis with complications. Nobody to attend to her. The doctor on call wouldn't go into the hospital, says it's filled with terrorists. And she doesn't laugh. Her lips must gum up when she pronounces the word. Her teeth must come loose. What a piece of shit. A tiny fear must be moving around in some remote corner of her, disturbing that all-too-serious air she balances while trying to look natural. The female guards come and go from the infirmary requesting that the sick *compañeras* give them guarantees they won't jump Dr. Cramer if she comes in to take a look at Patricia. The *compañeras* start to feel uneasy; they begin to feel the Chief of Security's filthy, uncut nails dig into their belly buttons. A doctor, male or female, or any other piece of shit, has never been jumped; they explain that to the guards who respond cow-eyed: "We don't know, that's what Dr. Cramer told us to tell you." And they leave. And they come back again with the same bullshit. The *compañeras* ask what kind of guarantee she wants, the guards say they don't know and return to talk it over with the doctor. And again: the doctor doesn't specify; she just demands her safety. "What safety?" the girls insist, and those faces of the guards, as if their heads had just been lopped off, come back with that tone of breaking the story of the day: "Safety. That's all."

This has been going on now for two hours. The *compañeras* propose being transferred to their wards so Patricia can be treated, and no sooner have the guards left with the offer than we see them return with those snaky mouths of theirs all puckered up to inform us that it's impossible, because the prison can't approve transfers of that sort without an order from above. And besides, there are three patients on i.v., impossible to move them. The *compañeras* say: "Who are they going to bother if they're laid up in bed?" to which the guards reply that we are guerrilla fighters, and that we always find a way, "that's why there's that war with guerrillas, that guerrilla war." "And besides," say the mercenaries, "you ladies don't know what it's like being caught in the middle, playing the role of the messenger." One of the women explodes: "In the middle of what, guard? You still haven't tried standing between the sword and the wall. Against that wall between the rifle and the firing squad. But history shows . . . you do know what history is?" And after an impatient sign from someone else: "We don't want to make trouble. We just want our *compañera* to get treatment."

I have to figure out in which hole I can hide this notebook this month. We're due for a shakedown any moment now.

19 May, in the morning, after breakfast

For five minutes I set aside the vegetable soup, which today is what this infamous box has become.

Maybe the only thing that keeps us awake at night is the middle of the summer, when the deadline for suffocation is extended only by breaking the order for silence, and I steal a smoke, prohibited after ten o'clock. It's incredible. But you talk and perspire less, you respond to a female guard with a tone of anger all built up in your intestines and January doesn't suffocate you so much. The only problem is that now it's autumn.

Last night: right after falling asleep we awoke as if going down on a sinking ship. From the ceiling we heard knocks that told us to answer the telephone. They gave us the latest: Patricia with her legs stiffening up, Doctor Cramer not budging from her position, the whole prison organizing to apply some pressure. The one informing us about the progress of Patricia's illness is another *compañera*, Amanda Sierra, a neurologist, who's sick but not so sick that she can't take time out to do something. So about an hour later, nine hundred out of the thousand and something of us that make up our wards—metal tins in hand but not yet banging them together—began to shout. We called out for the female guards, we asked to speak with the Chief of Security. No go. Then the banging began. We beat the cups into scrap metal. Dora hung back, silent, her eyes ringed, with a tin cup in her left hand but not banging it. She would go to the bathroom, pee, and then return to the activities, standing, her knees knocking together, gnashing her teeth, grinding them away just like when she sleeps. She pissed about ten times in three hours. But I'm not to be excused; to be honest, I was watching her closely.

Still nothing happened. We tried and tried, always without getting an answer. Then there was a decision to stop the clattering, very late at night. And we didn't have any more news other than what had already been given us at that time: Patricia was starting to experience stiffness in her arms and she was crying. Amanda had exhausted all means by which she could understand what was going on in the body of the *compañera*— she mentioned something about another disease working with the hepatitis—and the doctor left. The shifts changed and as soon as the new doctor took over he sent a message with the female guards, which they relayed:

"I know there is a doctor among the prisoners in the hospital. She should stop thinking about herself and help out her friend." The women, finding patience from I don't know where, sent him a message asking if he really thought that without any instruments or medicine Amanda could do any more than what she had already done. The guy sent a second message identical in length, content, and tone as the first one. The guards disappeared.

I wrote more than I thought I could.

Almost noon, same date

We got word from the second floor. Patricia's condition is critical. The Chief of Security ignores all requests to see him and the female guards didn't come near the hospital after the seven o'clock roll call. A male nurse came in and sedated the *compa-ñeras* with injections. They asked him to check in on Patricia and he didn't even look up. Amanda says that if Patricia doesn't receive immediate attention, meaning right now, in a few hours she'll go into a coma. No one is rattling the tin cups against the bars now, no one screams, they only make their request, firmly. The authorities are letting her die. When the female guards finished roll call in the hospital, Amanda talked to one of them and explained Patricia's condition. The guard gave her a sidelong glance and left quickly without making a sound. Amanda didn't really explain anything. She told her: "Our *compañera* is dying, guard."

20 May, about an hour after the morning roll call

It must have been somewhere between two and three in the morning when we were awakened by the voice of one of our cell mates who was screaming out at the prison personnel and all the neighbors in the surrounding area, letting them all know that Patricia Del Campo was dying without a choice due to lack of medical attention. In the middle of the night, her voice fell upon deaf ears.

Some of the *compañeras* went back to sleep. I had an urge to throw up but couldn't, and I stayed awake. The sun was coming up when I went back to sleep, and minutes later the female guards got us up for roll call.

We opened our eyes. Someone poked her head up and peeked out the window. I believe it was Telma. She said, "What's that," pointing toward the neighboring cell block. Some of us approached the window and saw dark clothing, black, blue, sticking through the bars. Someone said: "Crepe bands. Patricia died." Three or four of them, shaking their hands, their hair, saying that it couldn't be, it couldn't be. What the hell is it that couldn't be? A while ago, right after roll call, the same voice from the middle of the night, and then another, informed us of Patricia's death. It had happened between four and five o'clock. She was running a high fever and was delirious and choking. The *compañeras* at the hospital screamed, insisted, said: "Please, guard." When Patricia died, they sent word.

This time two male nurses and a female guard appeared, talking among themselves, dragging a gurney along with them. They slid open the gate, entering the hospital ward as if they were going to the corner market, laughing, going on about the pigeon-toed walk of another female guard. They placed her on the gurney and without looking at the rest of them they slowly wheeled her away. A few days back I regretted not having anything to say in this notebook. "So shitty," I had jotted down: "nothing to say." Or something to that effect.

The eyes see: they walk.

A Flat and Jaded Description of a New Year's Eve

I see the leg of the table and, shimmed between the leg and the floor, the piece of paper we had folded over several times to keep the table level. The dry, blistering wood, the old-green peeling paint, motionless under all our bored hands. I see the floor tiles, and the brass cylinder of a kerosene burner. A row of gray checkered blankets that extends to the entrance of the bathroom and Chana going into the bathroom, with her right hand reaching to undo her pants.

I see the edge of Teresa's bunk, magnified by the foreshortening caused by my face being pressed against the metal. I see the dirt building up in the grooves of the steel and I smell it. I know I must be inhaling it, but I can't tell. I know if I gave it a shot, I could leave Teresa's bed clean. Then the sneezes, and when the questions came I'd make up some story about allergies. But today is 31 December, and nobody thinks about organic alterations brought on by simple hardheadedness: I take a deep breath, I inhale, inhale all the way. But this task requires a great effort and it would be better if I just said no.

Inertia, inertia. Today inertia, just like most of yesterday. That delay. That oil in the soul.

I see the wall and I also smell it. I can smell the pale green color of the wall. Not pistachio, not mint. More like the bottom of our ocean littered with body parts. Better not stretch this one out.

Maura, Doña Maura walled in behind her mounting infinities. An infinity of rags, of newspapers, an infinity of acrimonies superimposed in her throat, against the ones she swallows several times every morning when she opens her eyes and discovers the ceiling. Because she sleeps on her back. There she blows. Today she bathed. Kept her promise. She said she would come to the table. She promised not to have a repeat of last year when she crawled back into bed as she saw the ward festivities getting under way, and that mess she managed to create afterwards. Now she's getting up. When her ass leaves the mattress the various piles of stuff all around her bounce up, spring up. See: there go the newspapers falling to the floor.

I see Maura's eyebrows join together over her nose. I see her teeth, few and far between and huge and dark, open up for the insult but I don't back down. My eyes bulge and I bear the obscenity of that face, that hair, those tits. All the excess.

I see María Clara mincing her steps toward the last bed—bed: bedsore, bedpan, bedbug—Maura's bed, to help her pick up the newspapers. But I also see her having second thoughts and retreating, repulsed by either Maura's hatred or her mustache or her hands, larded with braiding, breeding fatty tissue, and I don't know what disgusts her the most. She turns, I see her lower her head and bite her upper lip, take a few steps, rest the tip of her right foot against the foot of Flor's bed, play around with heel and toe, heel and toe on the floor.

I also notice Berta lovingly eyeing those metal plates, especially the ones holding slices of that marvelous sugar toast, a pure New Year's delicacy. She feels her tooth, looks at the plate, feels her tooth. It's been a month since she asked to see a dentist.

Maura seems to be putting the full weight of every one of her seventy years into keeping her mouth shut: I'm almost sure of it, because she's rocking her knee as she does when she's fighting off one of her more sordid impulses. And when I bring up these sordid impulses I'm not exactly sure what I'm referring to. But maybe right now really isn't the best time in my life to be reflecting on this subject; I just hope I don't end up more depraved than anyone else. That bare white knee: the so-what privilege of not having prison-issue pants for her measurements.

I look around and it's best that I don't see the expression on the lower part of Veronica's face: nose, mouth, and chin sagging heavily, near sleep. If she goes to bed I'll kill her. We'll kill her. She'd even get Maura to desert her.

I see the frilly edges of the plate with the large *pancocho,* that milkless and eggless bread pudding, the big one that took hours to confect. The metal banged into a dullness, the decorations made from sugar and water, I see the shine, the glistening in the sugary spirals that descend to the center of the dessert, making it disappear. It'd be best if the whole thing just vanished. It's not like we need this piece of work, this wonder conjured up by our culinary magic.

Martina cuts loose, showing off that fat she no longer has thanks to her goiter. Her eyeballs fly away from her, darting from one dish to the other, from the bars to Maura's stacks, to María Clara's hands—which barely move, they handle something wide, something thick, it looks like a compact fan, it could be a book, I can't quite make it out—to the base of the heater or to the floor tiles.

I see the edge of the wooden plank that supports our weight morning after morning of sitting or reclining on the bench, depending on the mood; I manage to trace the length of the crack in the middle, the one that snaps at our thighs and snags our uniforms. I see the edge, I see one side, the other end of the bench, the side Teresa's feet preferred; but today they're not on it: today is 31 December, today no one rests her feet on the bench.

Elizabeth. Mad, motormouth Elizabeth, I see her not able to forget, and certainly not today, the sixteen years of her sentence and her eighteen years of age, sixteen plus eighteen: thirty-four. I see her lead-gray T-shirt outlining her shoulders, her bones, two splintered sticks pointing up at the sky. After all, she thinks quite a bit about God, believes He's going to commute her sentence. Her limp, lifeless, almost childlike hair, as if nothing today, as if everything tomorrow. She still shows traces of her last bout with the flu.

The hour is drawing near. Maura is really burning up, looking like she's up to her dirty tricks. She sweats huge drops through her forehead. Her pores open, her skin is overrun with holes through which she vomits everything. Her veins, her stored-up fat, spilling out from everywhere, the world, the universe, her white, finite brain, Maura throws it all up.

She scares me. Exactly one year ago she got into it with Beatriz about something that was never made clear to anyone. And that's how we spent moving from the last day of an old year to the first day of a new one. That time Silvina pursed her lips. At one point she opened her mouth for some reason, I don't know what for, maybe not to have to say something that had been building up inside her, and I saw her white gums, whitened. She was scared.

Yes. The hour is drawing near. Chana closes in on the plate with the hors d'oeuvres, and from previous experience I don't think she'll go easy on them. Chana eats in a rage, as if trying to defend something she's about to lose forever. There she goes. In for the kill. I'd better get closer, or someone might notice the empty space.

There are several words that have been bothering me for some days now. They escape me. I'll have to think about them, conjure them up.

I sweat. My armpits are drenched. I feel faint, blood pressure dropping, words coming to me, over and over again. Pillaging, cannibalism. Acculturation. I don't feel good. Chana already took care of the plate. Veronica and Berta look at each other. They think the same thing. I sweat. My saliva goes bitter. Veronica and Berta always think the same thing. My ears go cold. My neck. Andrea and Griselda are late in joining the others. They talk, almost whispering, as if there were no other moments in their lives. Just now, when it's imperative that we mingle. My brow is dripping wet. I hope I get over this before somebody notices. Better not have any embarrassing moments on this December 31, at dinnertime. Grist for the piss-eye-chologists. Plenty of them. This isn't going away. And some of them even enjoy the approval of the majorities here. This crap, make it go away. Go away.

No luck. If I'm not careful they'll notice I'm missing. Maura managed to go over and stand by herself. It's not like gathering around the table is going to make us any happier. This old lady. Leticia can't resist the temptation and approaches her. She asks her—ha—she asks her to join the others, but of course it comes off sounding like a taunt. We can do without insults, Maura. No insults, please.

Dora parks her hips on the corner of the table and scans the entire ward inch by inch. She approaches this side (I must look pale, my lips are buzzing, my teeth are freezing), the words, the series, lineage, defoliation, eternal, the fear engulfs me, I don't want to faint, embarrassment, no embarrassments, not now, displacement, dichotomy, language and speech, my tongue that is falling asleep, that doesn't speak.

She's already looking this way, she'll discover me, she's looking. No, not yet; yes now. She sees me, I think she sees me.

Everyone is already eating. Except Maura. Elizabeth is practically sucking on a piece of something I can't quite make out, my vision is fuzzy, as if her anguish wouldn't allow her to take that bite.

Should I lower my head? I'll be too obvious if I start doing acrobatics. I need for somebody to lower my head. By myself, I'll try myself. Apply pressure, knees apart, and press my head down. Down. Now. Just like that. I feel a tingling in the back of my head. My eyes too. My ears. A sick bird in the clouds.

What does the bird do, what runs through its mind when it has reached the pinnacle of madness? It propels itself, flies, stops suddenly, hangs in midair, glides. It cranes its neck, stretching it out two, three times the length of its body, it twists its neck around, its head turns and turns, that neck is a screw made out of feathers, it extends its legs, retracts them, bends each joint, stretches and bends them. It lifts its tail, lowers it, shakes it, turns its whole body, its wings get tied up, caught up with its head, it's a mixture of flesh and feathers, dried flesh, hardened, a stone that has stopped in midair. And a stone doesn't just remain suspended. A stone weighs something, it follows the line of gravity and falls. A stone does just that: it falls.

Warmth returns to my body, my face. Get up slowly, Sara. I'm talking to you, you're so embarrassing. Come on, slowly, walk slowly but walk, just like that, yeah, get to the table, return to your friends, eat your hunk of *pancocho,* cheer up. Good thing you didn't decide to throw up, sweetie. Good thing.

Mingle with the girls. Lose yourself. Nobody noticed. Oh yes. Put that one in the books: nobody noticed. It's not going to kill you to be happy. Dora doesn't seem to have seen anything. Oh well.

They're all so close together. María Clara's elbow is rubbing against my right arm, Chana's hair clings to my shoulder, Flor's foot accidentally touches mine under the table.

Veronica looks at me, I smile at her because I'm sure she spots a shade of paleness in my face. I smile and hopefully manage to hide something with my grin. But I'm not trying to keep a straight face. I'm trying to keep this show of lack of composure under wraps because it's not a question of blowing my image. That's it: a collaboration with one's self. With one's own image. Because the book on me would be predictable: "Sara, petite bourgeoise with ideological weaknesses. Blood pressure drops during New Year's get-together." Very funny.

I see the large *pancocho,* now I see it up close, I see the center of the table with the great *pancocho* towering over the plates of sugar toast and hors d'oeuvres. I see fingers multiplied into infinite quantities. Flying, flitting fingers, fluid knuckles, speedy joints, voracious fingertips. Jumbled afterimages, threads of needs. The dented metal of the plates reflecting the light in the ward, so scarce, the scarce light, which during the last few hours we allow our brains to have, our so-festive brains.

In a corner of the floor over by the bars I see small gifts piled up, which, if tradition is followed, must be an assortment of small knitted, stuffed animals, manufactured clandestinely, and which will disappear for good after the first search of the year.

Leticia on the warpath. She chews on the bread with a seeming calm and a good deal of hatred. She feels like the pieces of *pancocho* are sticking their tongues out at her, that's the way they mock her, that's how they mock us all, mocking the little party we throw each year, mocking our will to laugh; and she gets revenge by chewing slowly, slightly crimping the left corner of her mouth, squinting her eyes. Swallowing, gulping it down her throat must be her real joy.

And Maura lying low, observing us. The rest of us around the table, the minutes passing and all of us going up to each other with hugs and tears.

What a drag. The Chief of Security approaches the bars and watches us, he sees us as monkeys making a royal mess. Time will tell who will be destined to make the great final mess. We turn around mechanically, looking at him as if he were a monkey making his own mess, an autistic and unqualified mess, and we turn our heads back around to the pieces of *pancocho*.

I see the legs of the Chief of Security beginning to move again, continuing his sweep through the wards, and I see the female guard who escorts him. I see all our thoughts, different, a little unbalanced.

I see the clamor, the bells, the explosions going off in the street; I see the street, a rat scuttling about, hunting a hole, and finally disappearing. And several blocks farther away a cat, destroyed by a party on wheels. A destroyed cat, out of its mind, I can see.

Congratulations, dear: you have one less year of prison left. Your brother is disappeared, not dead. There will be news. Your children are with your folks. Don't worry, yes, they do remember you, they know about your suffering, but they're not too bad off. Really. The chair we occupied in previous years on a night like this is now empty. Yes, your mother does look at it out of the corner of her eye, yes. But more than anything that just means she's trying to communicate with you at that very moment.

Maura looks at everything with a show of disgust. What to do? Approach her, wish her well? No. I'm not that crazy. I don't dare. Nobody dares.

Just one more piece of *pancocho.* Thanks.

The female guard marches through, checking off the corridor. She douses the lights. The sleep they deliver unto us.

Maura doesn't seem to be bothered. She has been pretending to be asleep for a few minutes now. Maura, Maura and her nerve, which allows her to pretend to be sleeping. Maura and her grudging hatreds, which let her get some sleep.

The letters fly.

Letter from Aubervilliers

Sara dear, my sister:

You just keep on insisting and insisting. Let's see if one of these days you'll give those of us who love you the hearty privilege of being the first to find out you've done away with that tendency of yours, as we would call it, to get all wound up in the most venerable metropolitan and patriotic tone. It's not that it bothers me (this is to shut your mouth and avoid that "I can't even count on my friend to listen to me") that you stir the pot, but you know I'm rather sensitive and would prefer, instead of stirring it, to put a lid on it. I repeat: whatever comes from you is received with all my love, but wouldn't it be better, even for a person of your complexity, to try to forget a little? I know, no one forgets anything. I know. But wouldn't it do you good to give yourself a vacation—a short one, yes—and enjoy the Los Angeles sun, the beaches of Santa Monica, those ebony rumps, the skies of the other hemisphere? Over there they don't have that constellation, the Three-Marías-I-get-the-one-in-the-middle,* as I'm sure you've discovered.

According to you there are wonders in California. When we shared that most elegant Ward 31, in times when our friendship was just beginning and I didn't suspect that your powers of conviction had malignant origins—remember, you pulled our legs, you tested the limits of people's naïveté or their sense of humor or their lucidity, narrating inventions that you made up as if they circulated through your blood—you laid one on me that I swallowed whole: the one about the extra-terrestrial beings that NASA kept secretly hidden in a museum in California. How did it go? I can almost remember, because your description was so juvenile I almost felt embarrassed for you. I could tell you'd grown tired of leading us on: enormous red eyes with a big zit on the back of their heads, where apparently their sexual organs functioned at full steam. I never got around to asking you how you were so well informed. In time you returned to the subject, as you usually do, and it just so happened that a cousin of yours who lived there had worked several years for the government

We enjoyed your deliberate lies, didn't we? We laughed. I suspect that now you laugh a little less. Me too. I tend to hide fears of everyday occurrences. Everyday, which is to say that Mauricio and the not-quite-one-year-old Paula are included. I hide my fears. I don't bare them to anyone: for me even the reflection would be enough to have them multiply.

Mauricio studies me too much. He observes me. I don't

---

* Refers to a cluster of stars seen only from the Southern Hemisphere. The term comes from a popular saying that young men direct to a group of young women: "Adiós a las tres Marías, la del medio es la mía." The sense in the context of the text is that in California you cannot see the three stars.

know what he wants, but he's always fixed on me. For reasons
I'm still not sure of, I can feel Paula drifting away from me.
(From me, her own mother, in case you don't remember.)

She distances herself with a gesture that is severe and grown
up for an eleven-month-old baby. She boards the ship, she waves
at me clutching (brandishing) a little pennant from I don't know
what country. Terrified, I don't respond. You don't know me as a
mother: I'm a retard, just awful. You could say I'm something of
a nun of motherhood. Vomit. An observation you may not quite
get: vomit is a product of the body; it is, in any case, respectable.
But no, wait: it's an inverse product, doing an about-face, turning back halfway there, a form of repentance, of indecision. So
yes, that's it: a nun of motherhood. Barf.

But look, I do what I can. My husband and daughter terrify
me, that much is sure. The child lives scandalously unencum-
bered. She moves those feet, trying to maintain her balance
with an air of conviction, so sure that balance is man's legacy,
believing that you achieve it merely by wishing for it. And her
father has pipe dreams of his own, and he also waves flags, his
little flags, for which I don't respect him any less. But I look at
him with such an air of "nobody home behind these eyes," and
for which the best result I get from him is an increasingly flag-
ging anger. Not even a forceful one anymore.

There I go whining again. You see? It's best not to stir
everything up, my friend. Let the matter follow its natural
course. Maybe I'll add some details in the next chapter, so as
not to alter the frequency of information.

The day when we can sit down and have a talk will be a happy
one, even though all the catching up is bound to get us down.

Five o'clock in the afternoon. I almost forgot: Gerardo and
Mariela popped up in Paris on their way to Barcelona. She

was as dark as she was when God set her loose on the earth, he was demeaning and omnipotent. She quiet, he all talky and jumpy. She with psoriasis, he sun toasted and sporting a gold chain around his neck. At least it wasn't a cross. Mariela avoided talking about prison the whole time. I prefer not to stir stuff up, but if something does come up, I don't hit the gas pedal. She, what can I tell you: she almost lets it be known explicitly that the subject really gets to her. Which hurts. She didn't understand it, or elaborate on it, or get over it. (Me neither, but that doesn't invalidate what I'm saying.) She didn't even change the subject, really. A shame. There was a moment I saw her lower her eyes when, I don't know at what point in the conversation, I was hit with the feeling that I was being invaded by the screams of our *compañeras* in the hole, calling out for water. Or asking to go to the bathroom. I don't know in what way you remember that echo, that sound. It's still so vivid to me. You once described it, on one of those mornings after hearing the screams go on all night, as being so many different things. I remember the images would come to you, different ideas, those screams really got your imagination going. They must have reinforced in you certain morbid, masochistic tendencies, because they set something off in you, they practically lit up your eyes in the darkness as you listened. Not from happiness of course. It was as if during that time you were capturing an essence, the essence of everything, the most crucial, the most exact essence, and you would have blocked out everything around you to concentrate on enjoying, on relishing the moment—the hours—of emotion.

And I suffered, unable to move. My head buried under a pillow, groping for all kinds of useless reflections. This sounds out of place. Better that way, you would say, if it's out of place.

Things that are where they should be don't interest me: they're left exposed to being found and destroyed.

Midnight. Around eight o'clock I went for a walk with Paula. I put her in the stroller and we went out. It was rather brisk out on the street. I purchased some coffee, cigarettes, and a carton of milk. Then we came back in. I didn't know what to do. Paula had fallen asleep, so I flipped on the television. After the 9:30 news there was a program on the current state of children's literature here. A busty brunette came on talking about various books by French authors written for ages eight to twelve. Just about everything she mentioned I was unfamiliar with, but suddenly she goes and refers to a book by a certain Josephine Colomb: *La fille de Carilés.* She went on about the plot and as I was listening I felt like I was seven years old, I could practically see the humidity stains on the bedroom walls of my childhood home, me rubbing my eyes and nostrils against the sheets to drown out my sobbing brought on by the emotion of imagining Carilés all alone, days before she would find Miguita. I was terrified—listening to this woman—by the possibility that even though I was here in Europe and 34 years old, my mother would come right through the bathroom door and enter my bedroom to turn off the radio just at the moment when Nicola Paone's "The Coffee Pot" was moving me the most.

La fille de Carilés. Telling you this, one could almost reproduce a kind of notice from Atlantida Press (you too must have devoured the Billiken series back then), which would state that the author was imparting "a profound lesson in humanity" with her story. And talking about the "principles that guided" the collection, it would list (by that time the enumeration had already pulled copious tears from me): moral refinement, healthy, young optimism, confidence in the triumph of noble sentiments.

And in the same series of little books there was a terrifying *Santa Rosa de Lima,* so saintly that she was never stung by mosquitoes and whom the trees, stooping over, would greet as she passed by, *Journey to the Ranquel Indians, Cromwell, Taras Bulba, Ivanhoe,* and *Tartarin of Tarascon.*

I relish tasting again what remained as the dregs of my childhood. Don't envy me so much. It's not a bad thing to be able to stick out your hand to that during certain moments of adult hopelessness, but this all has more to do with a rather vulgar kind of peace, I swear. You would find a way not to experience it, you sick, twisted thing you. Anyway, your own history doesn't afford you many chances to come up with ways to let your imagination just relax.

But look, Carilés's daughter didn't seduce me. Sure, I was a little jealous of her luck, although later, without reflecting on it too much I saw that I was no weakling and even less a circus owner. To own something so beautiful—even if for you circuses are details from hell—you've got to know how to live or how to die. I'm totally incapable in both respects. To be a circus owner or to inherit a circus would have been too overwhelming. I don't deny that imagining the thousands of sparkling and dazzling dresses to be worn on stage, which, according to my rough calculations, Miguita had at her disposal, I came up with the grand idea of mounting a circus in my house, supposing that with a circus there, my parents would no longer be able to refuse to set me up with the appropriate wardrobe.

Don't laugh, dummy. Maybe it wasn't you that made up—as usual—that bit about being Cleopatra's descendant, amusing yourself by telling it to anyone who would listen to you? One thing, though: I used to ask myself if by the time men reach

sixty their sexual organs have shriveled up yet, thinking about
the lonely life that old man Carilés led, and was sure that his
piece was more or less already shot.

Almost four days later.

It's a good thing that here no one goes out and sweeps the
sidewalk. One of the advantages of being an exile in France:
you don't have to sweep the sidewalk.

The following day.

It's nine o'clock in the morning. The job in the restaurant
fell through. More than falling through, though, I boycotted it
with the excuse of those guilty feelings of a mother who leaves
her child in a nursery. All it took was for me to tell the owner
that I had a kid. Don't answer me with your smart talk, do me
that little favor.

Three o'clock in the afternoon.

Back to Gerardo and Mariela, I mean, to the conversation in
which I mentioned the girls in the isolation cells.

I wasn't trying to be all doomy and gloomy, but if it's there
it just comes out all by itself. I gradually broached the subject
without employing any real strategy, just as Mariela was buttering one of her two pieces of toast: the same two pieces as
always, the exact same two. I think she's been eating the same
two pieces of toast with black tea since prehistoric times, especially since she belongs pretty much to that stage of evolution.
(No; I mean, you know I care for her, but it really irks me that
she doesn't muzzle that husband of hers she still keeps around.)

I'll continue: she was buttering her toast and I said something to her along the lines of: it's a good thing there's no
water shortage here. (In connection with the crack the ever-

glib Gerardo made about the three small plants in my windowsill—the ones in the picture I sent you—.)[1] Something went off inside of her. And it showed *plenty* (that's what the Chileans settled in and around Paris say) because she bit her lips in a very conventional way. That's when I really got angry with her and pressed the matter.

But tell me: what were those noises? What sounds were they? You used to talk about birds with black feathers, with their beaks cut off, remember? Chopped off with axes, you used to say. Out of those nubby mouths came sounds that spread through the Villa Devoto night. There was an echo. And the wind twisted the sound and changed it up. It came to us neutral you said, neutral just like everything in real life that's passed from one state to the other. And it scared you. You shook and the hairs on your body stood on end because the screams reached Ward 31 like a shapeless sound, transformed; you thought about those carnival nights and became terrified.

There were eighty of them or more, and for hours they asked for "Water, guard, please, we're thirsty," and that phrase reached our brains like a long "uuuuuu," which fluttered in the air way above our heads, in the night, with no way to condense itself into a concrete sound.

It scared us, Sara. That's the truth. But it wasn't easy to admit. The lamp turned on even though it's daytime smacks me right in the pupils. My eyes close all by themselves. I believe that granting myself a little nap as a reward wouldn't offend anyone. And even less my little soul buddy, although she would rather see me with my nose in one of Hauser's three weighty tomes, or undertaking some similar form of suffering. Catch you later.

7:20 in the evening. I finally fell asleep, but the delicate, sweet, infernal crying of my just as sweet, delicate little girl didn't take long to turn my dreams into a blur of baby bottles and comings and goings. And did time fly until just now.

I think Mariela must have wound up tossed in the hole close to ten times in three years. She defended our interests well, fought for them. She ended up being punished out of her sheer conviction in what she was doing. The guilt that played out in the others didn't affect her much. She didn't need atonement: she didn't feel guilty for being alive or for not going to the cells every now and then. When she listened to Florencia (remember?) reciting that poem—Florencia was joking, of course—that poem by I don't know who that went something like "into this world we are born to suffer . . . " she turned green. You'd probably say she turned green because it bothered her, and if it bothered her it was because she wasn't convinced it wasn't like the poem said. But that's your own hang-up: you can't tell me anything; the Atlantic ocean separates us. And in my complete defense. Besides, what I say is true.

I only ask myself what's wrong with her now, why doesn't she want to bring up the subject of solitary and all those thirsts (thirst can be plural, as I'm sure you're aware, dear), why would she be bothered by that when she doesn't appear to have changed all that much? Each trip to the hole, for at least fifteen days.

And now here, or in other places in the world. I mean her or anyone: you, me, the others, remembering, wanting or not wanting to butter those noggins of theirs with memories.

Eleven at night. I'm wide awake. That is to say, I'm not sleepy. But I've had it with worrying about you today. I'm going to curl up to a movie on television. Last week they showed *Psycho* (Anthony Perkins) around this hour or later, and my little girl sleeping and Mauricio gone. I spent hours somewhere between panic and then pretending not to panic, and neither the commercials nor the bananas made me feel any better. We'll see what they reveal tonight. Greetings to the ones over there. I'll write again in a few days. Kisses.

Juliana.

P.S. Have that kid of yours already. I think it's about time. [1]—In my next letter I'll try not to bunch punctuation signs together. I think they're pretty useless.

I walk. I stop: I walk.

A Way Back

It was so hard to look up without hearing a scream that reminded us all that we were still prisoners, but it was even more
difficult to overlook the five o'clock in the morning pitch, starry
sky. I raised my eyes just as my foot hit the platform of the
military bus.

The sky was exactly like that: black and filled with stars.
Three years and three months without seeing the nighttime sky.
That distance, so concrete, which can be established between the
nocturnal sky and night itself, the condition of being nighttime
for the days, for the years. But I write it down now, I said it
months later. Though at the moment of shielding myself from
that freedom that was falling upon me, I didn't think or say a
thing. Maybe it occurred to me that I was, after all, still alive
and that another alternative at that very instant would have been
the rain. Nothing that somebody else couldn't have thought of.
To cross that space between the prison and the military bus in

the rain. Three steps under water. Good title, if I were telling this story.

What I'm doing just isn't working, trying to describe a moment of that magnitude. Almost absurd. Possible, but absurd. And let this be a sterile clarification: I believe in the word. Fervently. For so many who can't even imagine certain realities, who have passed through zones so distant from actual experience, or who haven't passed through any zone at all, there's no recourse other than words that are heard, read. Images or no images, always the word.

But a movie would be ideal: that darkness in a space that's open but enclosed, a row of women—one of them getting on the bus and stumbling because she was looking up at the sky—. Bags slung across shoulders, legs out of shape.

There is a fear that paralyzes me now, always that same one of not being able to find the right expression, the suitable one. Fears. Unjustified, because an expression without objections doesn't exist. To the point that the most enjoyable aspect of the manipulation, the most anguishing and rewarding part of the literary kneading process is to replace one word with a better one. Although you can use absolutely the worst word or one nearly as poor, or one not so poor but oddly irreplaceable. And those are the limits. And the most aggravating part.

I don't know who was in front of me in the line of released prisoners. Nor who was behind me. After peeking at the sky as if looking at it through a keyhole, I boarded the bus. The rear seats were empty, I went for the widest one, with the big window completely at my disposal. Three other *compañeras* sat down alongside me. All three had the same possibility I did, to turn their heads around and look behind them.

I clutched my freedom bag. I pressed it against my right hip with my elbow. I had saved two notebooks with two years' worth of notes from the searches.

I know that once seated, still hoping for the okay to smoke during the trip, I looked down at my feet. Now I can't remember what shoes I was wearing. I don't know what I saw, but I stared there for just an instant. I was always fascinated by the tips of my shoes. That would happen when after long tense periods I would feel relieved, or when something uncertain would become more clear. I believe that this time, in a particularly heightened state of sensations and risks, I was handing myself over to life or death as they both came, if they came (it had to be one or the other: everything indicated that we were about to crash through the barrier of inertia), with or without sounds, pains, colors, or shapes. I looked at the tips of my shoes. They must have been black moccasins, worn out. I imagined them dragging across the promenade on Córdoba Street and I felt like I was confusing everything, because my family's intolerance would never allow me to enjoy a soft pair of old shoes; instead they would force me to endure a brand new pair. Any other possibility would be to offend my progenitors in their poor-parents-of-a-terrorist condition.

I looked at my shoes and wiggled my toes in spite of the tight fit. Just to get them to swing to the new rhythm.

We waited for the authorization to smoke. One of the officers who kept watch over us inside the bus recommended that we not get up from our seats and said, "You can smoke if you wish," and twenty-nine matches crackled in unison.

We were heading down the highway toward Rosario. The dawn came up screaming. For some strange reason a few of the *compañeras* had fallen asleep. Outside the light was tawny colored and we had to look at it. There were cars going in the other direction. Cars: we had to look at them. Tires, bumpers, and if possible, steering wheels. Cars. Sounds of freedom, a blur of colors, all mixed together.

Billboards. The ubiquitous Coca-Cola, each time more red and white, more visible and brilliant over the last few years. A bird, which was probably a sparrow, had alighted on the top of the sign, which then became a blue sky, the verdant Argentine countryside, a Coca-Cola sign, and a bird. Nothing. Nothing really. And the synthesis of everything.

I said to the one on my left "Go on and take a look." "Coca-Cola sign," she said, opening her eyes and scrutinizing me in an attempt to get closer, to understand my surprise. I was probably wrong, but I felt I couldn't say anything else.

Something turned inside of me. A corner of my brain rotated and settled in a new position. And everything else that came along seemed to me to be a lie. How could all those living trees be real, those cornfields, those shadows? There was only one truth and that was jail, the state of confinement. As we headed down the road that idea dug itself in: I had to remain calm. I couldn't allow myself to scream out of happiness; nobody—and even less the *milicos*—would understand. But if everything was uncertain, if the reality was something else and this was only some technicolor movie, whatever provoked the happiness would vanish, and with the sketchy remains would come a peace.

The bus slowed. It stopped. The military bus that was transporting us back to freedom was now sitting in the middle of the countryside. We looked at each other, we didn't ask each other a thing. We saw a service station, and an officer said, "Hit the bathroom." And they kept watch over us two at a time. I know I stepped into mud with my old shoes and I liked it. It was like warming up my legs with a land fire, not one from underground. Cold, but fresh mud. Just like stepping barefooted on some skeleton popping out of nowhere, getting all tangled up in its ribs, my feet plunging between its vertebrae; possible. Why not? A little desperate. Like entering into a voluntary period of mourning, into a clot that works away in the throat to prevent happiness from spreading, that prevents you from putting it to good use. I wanted to find something to say about the mud, but before I could open my mouth I was sure that it was a lie. That the mud, if it really was mud, didn't belong to me.

I raised my head up on the way to the bathroom and I saw a sky that was intensely blue and alien; I pulled down my panties and urinated in a small, shabby room, so typical but missed during these recent times. You can, of course, come to miss a service station bathroom in this country. The noise of the urine splattering against the bowl made me feel like laughing, and since I was alone I laughed. I avoided really cracking up though. I told myself: noises are for being heard, but let's not exaggerate. Besides, in the Villa Devoto latrines you can also hear people peeing. And that's what matters.

I wiped off the drops of urine and pulled up my panties. The "freedom" panties. Which freedom, I asked myself. I was done. I opened the bathroom door feeling bad. I would have stayed there alone a few moments longer. And I'd say that I stayed behind sitting on the toilet with just my wishes, my head resting against the left wall, my eyes open and staring at a bucket full of bloody sanitary napkins, which had been there for some time, while in reality I was leaving the bathroom and getting on the bus as another *compañera* dropped her pants in the solitude of the service station bathroom.

We were on the road again. Almost halfway there. Rosario closed in on us cardboard-like. Prop-like. The light was of yellow painted paper and the buildings got shorter each step of the way. The closer we got, the more it seemed we were about to crash into a stage mounted a foot and a half off the ground. Transportable, as mobile as my own feeling about life, or death.

That morning was now over and it was a rough one. We arrived. We went inside. We saw ourselves—I saw myself—as puppets being led toward the command post of the II Army Corps, walking toward a side door, crossing a street.

Standing in files in that courtyard, the Chief of the II Corps reminding us that the mistakes made by him and his men were easily repeatable; the usual sermon: the threat, a little more fear.

In the middle of this fiction, I hazily remember the street and my mother with a flower bouquet that I never understood, and the assault vehicle in which three of the twenty-nine prisoners were transported to the police headquarters where our freedoms under surveillance would take shape.

And while we waited for the police in charge to finish filling out the forms and signing them, that door to the office fronting the room we were in cracked open, allowing that skinny guy to leave, that one who, in the middle of the summer heat, with those gasping sounds, appeared with that jacket, the best one

Hugo had owned years ago, the one he stole from the closet on the day they took me away, the guy wearing it as if from that first moment he'd never taken it off. He appeared through one door and disappeared out another, without looking but knowing that I saw him.

And I remembered later that other street, the one we could see from my father's car on the way to his house and the cats. It was already four o'clock in the afternoon.

I got to thinking and told myself: you're young, darling. You're not even twenty-five yet. You can still see the traffic lights, the trees, and the men who manage not to get run over by a motorcycle as they cross the street. And the ones who don't quite make it. You're fit for feeling and not feeling. Enjoy the rare virtue of getting angry when you don't get your way and then when you're always forgiven afterwards. You're torn between the urge to write and the urge to urinate. You still belong to that group of people who wake up at four o'clock in the morning with some idea and decide to snap on the light and write it down at the expense of spending the next day all worn out. Don't worry about those jackets, which would accomplish their objective if you only let them. Blot them out. Conjure them up. They're ghosts. And ghosts are real only when you want them to be. Come on. Jackets are no big deal. They don't exist. Remember that you enjoy certain privileges: a nice face, a good sense of humor. Take advantage of them. A lively and alert brain. Exploit it. Now you can see the world. You can put yourself right in the middle of it, you can be a real ball-busting, in-your-face person, which is what turns you on the most, what moves you the most. So don't get all worked up. Don't get caught up in the silence, or against it. Speak and don't speak.

Listen and blow off whatever it is you don't want to hear. Laugh and don't laugh. And don't screw around. Do whatever you feel like doing and don't do it. Take a deep breath. Come on. Let the air enter. Enter. That's what I told myself on my way to the cats. On my way back.

Photo by Paloma Marugan

Alicia Kozameh is a writer living in Los Angeles. Born in Rosario, Argentina, she is currently at work on her fourth novel.

David E. Davis, originally from Texas, now resides in Los Angeles, where he teaches language and translates fiction.

Saúl Sosnowski is Professor of Latin American Literature, and Director of the Latin American Studies Center at the University of Maryland.

Compositor: G & S Typesetters, Inc.
Printer: Thomson-Shore, Inc.
Binder: Thomson-Shore, Inc.
Text: 11/15 Granjon
Display: Granjon